18/2/94

To Harpreet,

You're the first

Sikh to read one of my

books — hope you like it.

Best Wishes,

Roddy

Roddy O'Sullivan

The Horrific Secret of Westport House

© 2023 **Europe Books**| London
www.europebooks.co.uk | info@europebooks.co.uk

ISBN 9791220145725
First edition: December 2023

The Horrific Secret of Westport House

Dedicated to the memory of the wonderful, ever-shining,
Deirdre Hughes [1955 – 2023]

WESTPORT HOUSE
[Credit: Westport House]

Westport House is one of the few privately-owned historic houses left in Ireland. Long associated with Ireland's Pirate Queen, Grace O'Malley [1530 – 1603], the House is sited on 400 acres of mature woods amid rolling Mayo countryside and enjoys unsurpassed views of Croagh Patrick, Clew Bay and Clare Island.
[TOURIST GUIDE TO Co MAYO 2021]

Chapter 1

"What will I do now?" muttered Shane Donnegan, his eyes sweeping the busy Arrivals Terminal.

He set down his suitcase and, realising his phone was dead, tried to dismiss the same fears that had haunted him since first boarding the Airbus 350. *What if Aunt Agnes and Uncle Lionel's car breaks down?* he thought. *They won't be able to contact me...*

Jet-lagged and trying to decide whether he was more awake than asleep, he removed the *Qantas Airlines – Unaccompanied Minor* tag from around his neck. He hoped someone might make eye contact with him because his name wasn't on any of the placards being held aloft in the waiting crowd. His Dad was forever telling him how chirpy and friendly the Irish were, but everyone seemed just as grumpy as in the other airports he'd stopped at during the long flight. He shivered in his t-shirt and jeans, realising that European summers were far colder than back home.

"Shane!" The piercing cry made him swing around.

Oblivious to those around her, a small, grey-haired woman was waving and pushing her way through the crowd. "It's me!" she called. "Your Aunt Agnes."

Relieved the wait was over but unsure of what to say to this smiling, tear-stained stranger, he could only mumble, "G'day, er, Aunt Agnes."

"Let's be having a look at my long lost great-nephew." She dried her eyes then held him at arm's length. "And just listen to yourself; you sound like you've just stepped off a plane from Australia."

"Maybe because I... just have."

"Oh, you know what I mean. You look much older

than fourteen; you so remind me of your poor mother, Finnoula." She crossed herself. "God rest her soul."

Shane felt his face glow as his Aunt enveloped him without warning in an embrace which seemed to last for an eternity.

"I'm making a holy show of myself." Staring at him with mock severity, she added, "This isn't the Australian outback. Haven't you a jacket or something?" She turned to the tall, thin man standing to attention nearby. "Lionel, you remember Shane?"

Bowing his grey head, Uncle Lionel said, "Hardly, m'dear, it's been, er, ten years?" He proffered his hand. "Welcome back, Shane. Good flight?"

"Yes thanks, Uncle."

"Good firm handshake there, m'boy. Remember, keep your back straight; look the world in the eye. How's your father's leg coming along?"

"Once they take off the plaster, he'll visit me here."

Shane became aware of another figure standing close by, a hardback under his arm. About Shane's age, he was chewing contentedly and from behind rimless glasses, his eyes were focused unwaveringly on Shane.

"This is Finbar McAuley, our genius engineer," introduced Aunt Agnes. "We call him the Professor; he goes to your new school, St Columbanus, and…"

"… G'day to you, cobber," interrupted Finbar, his phoney Australian accent almost flawless.

"G'day to you, Finbar," said Shane.

"Lay off the Finbar stuff, everyone calls me Tubs on account of my…" He winked and tapped his ample waistline. "… Ice cream-heavy bones, understand?"

I like this guy, Shane thought. *No way would he make the fourth football team, but there's something*

14

impish about him...

"Shall I take your suitcase, Shane?" said Uncle Lionel.

"I'm fine, Uncle, thanks all the same."

Exiting into the morning air, Shane stopped to take in his new surroundings. For a few precarious seconds he tingled with a weird sensation of having experienced the identical situation before, somewhere in the buried past, in some prior time or existence. The feeling was so vivid that he momentarily felt unsure of where he was. Or even who he was. *Everything feels spooky or unreal or... something...* he thought.

"All right, m'boy?"

"Er, it's just things feel sort of, well, strange."

"As one would expect; new faces, new places. Let's get the column moving. It's a long trek to Clew Bay Lodge."

***

Shane's black eyes stared out of the window as the Renault Clio manoeuvred into the slow-moving Dublin traffic. He'd half expected empty country lanes yet here he was, bumper to bumper in a traffic jam far worse than in Brisbane.

"I'd rather hand-to-hand combat," said Uncle Lionel, blowing through his moustache, "than face morning rush hour."

Aunt Agnes patted his shoulder. "Watch the blood pressure, dear; it's not the Falklands."

Uncle Lionel muttered something unintelligible under his breath.

I see Macca's are called McDonald's here, Shane thought. *I wonder will they have my favourite sausages?*

15

No Aussie Rules football but... He pointed. "Say, it's over two hundred and fifty kilometres to Westport."

Aunt Agnes turned around sharply. "That signpost was in Irish; I didn't know you could speak Gaelic?"

"I can't."

"You must have learnt it at some point."

"If I did, I don't remember."

She nodded knowingly. "You learnt it from your mother; that's the answer obviously."

"Er, can I ask you about Mam, Aunt Agnes?"

"Of course, dear."

"I'm looking forward to making new friends and that, but I'd like to know something about my early years here with Mam – before I left for Oz."

"What's stopping you asking your father?"

"He's always so vague."

"I see."

"I've never seen a photo of me as a toddler; no blowing out birthday candles or, well, anything. All I have is this ring she left me." He stretched his ringed finger towards Aunt Agnes. "It's my only memento of her."

"Umm, queer-looking thing. I'm sure she had enough on her plate without being bothered with taking photographs and the like. Isn't that right, Lionel?"

"Harrumph."

Dad and me waved goodbye to Ireland after Mam passed away, he thought. *The only place I remember is Oz, yet somehow everything feels so familiar, so green...*

Tubs' mock-adult accent broke through his thoughts. "Why," he asked with exaggerated seriousness, "come all this way to an Irish school?"

"Dad reckons it'll, er, keep my head out of the clouds. He doesn't want me slogging my life away on his fishing boat, like I do most summers. What's this St

Columbanus like?"

"It's fulltime; it's a weekly boarder; or it's a day school. I'm on a scholarship; no way could Mum afford the fees on her supermarket wages."

"What about your dad?"

"They're separated," muttered Tubs, wistfully regarding his trainers before adding quickly, "As I was sayin', St Columbanus is a Monday to Friday place unless you're a nutjob who's into sport." He deliberately spat out the word sport.

Shane playfully elbowed him. "I'm afraid I'm one of those."

"When do you start?"

"I have the interview and exam tomorrow and if I pass…"

"…Of course you'll pass," Aunt Agnes cut in.

Tubs' accent reverted to Australian. "That's real ripper, blue."

"How come you know Strine, so well, er, Tubs?"

"What's Strine?"

"It's the funny way we speak English back home."

Tubs proffered a bag of toffees. "I loved those old Aussie soaps − *Home and Away* and *Neighbours* − so, I became a world expert in Strine."

Despite his best efforts, Shane's grip on the conversation was slipping; the long journey was taking its toll. "I'm sort of bushed, folks," he said, stifling a yawn.

"Finbar, pull that rug over him," fussed Aunt Agnes. "We don't want him catching his death of cold on his first day back."

Shane's last recollection of the journey was Aunt Agnes saying, "Chalk and cheese those two are, Lionel, yet it looks like they're going to be great friends. Mm, now that I think about it – I've never seen a photo of Shane as a toddler, never mind a baby…"

Chapter 2

Shane awoke staring at the ceiling, unsure of where he was. His nightmare had been more vivid than usual – the same passageway, that door, the horrific darkness. Trying to shake off the clammy feeling of unreality that clung to him like glue, he commanded himself to breathe more easily… *I remember the air stewardess shaking me, saying my cries were disturbing other passengers…*

"Wakey, wakey, Shane." Aunt Agnes was at the bedroom door. "Breakfast in twenty minutes."

Tossing the sleep from his eyes he called, "Thanks, Aunt Agnes."

Ten minutes later he was staring at his reflection in the bathroom mirror, hardly recognising himself in white shirt and tie, teeth gleaming and his black hair neatly sleeked backwards. *I look like a posho; nobody would notice my slightly crooked nose.* Through the window, he saw for the first time how the sea and sky were dominated by volcano-shaped Croagh Patrick, its tiny church gleaming whitely on the summit. *That distant blob on the horizon must be Clare Island; it reminds me of a whale's hump… those rashers and sausages smell great…*

Aunt Agnes smiled as he entered the kitchen. "My, oh, my, Shane, you do look smart. Are we a wee bit nervous this morning?"

"Yes, a bit."

"Your bedroom is also your study. If you need a break from your old aunt and uncle, you have your own computer."

"Thanks, Aunt Agnes. That's really great."

As Shane took his place at the table, Uncle Lionel cleared his throat. "A short exam isn't worth getting

19

nervous about, eh? I remember once, my platoon was…"

"…I don't think that Shane wants to hear about your Army days, dear."

"Maybe later, Uncle," said Shane, attacking the breakfast. "I don't have time right now."

"Remember, a headmaster is like a regimental sergeant major; everything must be spick and span." He leant across to flick something off Shane's collar. "Ha, ha, dust. That looks better."

"Thanks, Uncle."

"Before I drop you off, m'boy, have a browse around your new home; it takes a bit of getting used to."

Shane quickly discovered that Clew Bay Lodge wasn't a house, it was a sprawling mansion. He lost his way twice during his exploratory walkabout before eventually finding his way back to the main dining room. Feeling slightly awed beneath the high ceiling and long mirrors, he felt like walking on tiptoe so as not to disturb the severe-looking men in uniform who stared down at him from the large wall-portraits. *So different from Dad's cramped Brisbane flat*, he thought. *Oops, I'd better call him before we head off for St Columbanus…*

"Hi, Dad, sorry I couldn't ring yesterday, I…"

"…No probs, son. Settling in OK?"

"Yeah, really well. Clew Bay Lodge is great. Dad… er, do you know if I've ever been able to speak… Irish?"

"That's a strange thing to ask."

"I know. But did I… ever?"

"Of course not. You hadn't even gone to school before you and me arrived in Oz."

"Mam didn't teach me?"

"If she did it would have been a miracle. She didn't have a word of Irish. Do you want to learn it or

something?"

"No... I was just... just wondering. How's the leg?"

"The plaster won't come off for a while. Oh, hell, the American evening group has just arrived. Call you back later, OK?"

"OK, Dad. Bye"

"Miss you, son. Bye."

***

As Shane met Tubs outside the school gates, a line of flash mountain bikes braked alongside. From the lead machine, the muscular leader turned and made a muffled wisecrack over his shoulder to his cronies which produced an explosion of raucous laughter.

"That's Jeremy Brockenhurst," whispered Tubs, biting his lip, "the school's weight-liftin' champ. His dad's a school governor. I call him Pot Hole."

"Why?"

"Because everyone tries to avoid potholes in the road."

Brockenhurst was pointing at Shane. "So you're the latest blow-in?" he said, his lip curling.

"What's it to you?" said Shane, coldly holding Brockenhurst's gaze.

"What kind of an accent is that?" said Brockenhurst, pushing his Ray-Ban sunglasses to his forehead.

"Australian."

"Umm, I thought you sounded aboriginal."

As Brockenhurst's followers sniggered, they parted to allow the Deputy Head through, struggling under an armful of books. Cannily sensing trouble in the air,

21

Mr Stubbs said, "You've no business in the junior school, Brockenhurst. Move on." Fussily ushering everyone forward, he asked, "You're Shane Donnegan?"

"Yes, sir."

"I'm your exam invigilator. I'll see you in the Classics Block, 9.15."

"Thanks, sir."

As Mr Stubbs departed, Brockenhurst pointed again at Shane, thumb cocked behind his finger, like it was a gun. "There's something about you that pisses me off," he said before accelerating away, followed by his pack of hyenas.

"Nice one, fella," came a deep voice from behind.

Two other pupils had overheard the Brockenhurst exchange, one tall and burly; the other thin and whippet-like. The bulkier guy addressed Shane. "Anyone who stands up to bullyboy Brockenhurst is a friend of ours. I'm Mike Tarpey and that there's Peter Woods; you'll be in our class." He held out his hand.

"Hi, Mike, I'm Shane Donnegan."

"Nobody calls him Mike," said Peter, shaking hands. "Everyone calls him Caveman, the reason's obvious."

"And nobody calls him Peter," said Caveman, rubbing his stubbly chin, "everyone calls him Scruffy, the reason's obvious."

"Scruffy?" said Shane, frowning as he clocked Peter's cufflinks and suede shoes. "I don't get it."

"Unlike the other meatheads around here," said Peter with a knowing grin, "I know how to dress properly."

Tubs pulled Shane's sleeve. "Don't be late."

"See you around, fella," called Caveman as he and Peter sauntered off.

Tubs frowned. "You make friends real easy, Shane. I've been here for two years and those guys hardly ever speak to me. What's the secret?"

Shane placed an arm around Tubs' shoulders. "We'll make friends together."

"Thanks, Shane."

I've made a friend already... also made myself an enemy.

As they approached the main building, a tall, dark-skinned girl broke away from a nearby group of girls. "Hiya, Finbar," she greeted, "what was all that with Brockenhurst?"

"He was givin' Shane stick about bein' an Aussie and Shane stood up to him, that's what."

She looked around to take in Shane. "Well, I'm glad to see someone finally taking a stand against that eejit. He's got such a big mouth. Hey, girls, wait! Bye, Finbar."

Tubs beamed at her disappearing figure. "Hear that, Shane? She called me by my proper name."

"What do you mean?"

"Some people call me things like porky, fatso – I'm not used to bein' called Finbar."

"Why not just try and forget about it? If they don't get a reaction, maybe they'll leave you alone."

"I've got to hand in homework to Stubbs; catch you up in a few minutes."

On his way to locate the Classics Block, Shane recognised the same attractive girl Tubs had spoken to. Scrutinising her face in a hand mirror behind one of the colonnades, she was applying finishing touches of eye-liner.

"Excuse me," Shane began pleasantly. "I'm trying to find the…"

She snapped the mirror closed and head high, flounced past. "Find it yourself," she said.

Shane was still standing open-mouthed as Tubs reappeared. "Who was that, Tubs?" he said, indicating the girl's departing figure.

"Zara Singh," said Tubs grimly, "Westport's answer to Bollywood. She's in our class, one of the twenty girls here; she teaches your Uncle Lionel how to use a computer."

"She's one seriously sour Sheila."

"A friend of hers recently scooted back to Oz with Zara's ivory chess set; a present from *papa* − he's some bigwig businessman − so she has a thing about Aussies."

"What's that got to do with me?" said Shane indignantly.

"That's Zara. Her mother's worse; yakkidy yakkin' about *our* Zara's actin' class and *our* Zara's el-o-cution class and how wonderful *our* Zara is at chess and art." With a malicious grin, he added, "That nettle could annoy a crowbar into singin' hymns. Hey, you're right outside the exam block. Good luck."

Chapter 3

Shane continued to stand stiffly in front of the Head's desk. Hatchet-faced Mr Stubbs waited in close attendance, staring fixedly at his shoes. Only the scratching of Mr Hoskins' antiquated fountain pen broke the thick silence while he pointedly continued writing. Finally he looked up, and feigning mild surprise said, "Your interview was satisfactory, Master Donnegan." The hint of a smile playing around the corners of his eyes disappeared.

Shane shuffled under the teachers' combined gazes. *Why the Darth Vader looks?*

Mr Hoskins' grey eyes stared straight ahead over his half-moon glasses. "Your written results are somewhat different." He allowed his phlegmy cough to subside before reaching for the open folder on the desk. "Biology 61%, maths 59%. Ah, history…" His hawk-like eyes glinted as he dramatically let the folder drop. "You scraped a bare pass." An iron note in his voice, he added, "If you wish to attend St Columbanus, may I expect some revision in the subject during the summer?"

It wasn't really a question, it was a command.

"Absolutely, sir."

Mr Hoskins consulted the folder again. "But it's the Greek marks that are so extraordinary." He removed his glasses, quickly wiped and resettled them.

Shane's heart sank. *I shouldn't have had a go at that Ancient Greek! I'd only done two months of it back in Brisbane…*

Hoskins icily regarded Mr Stubbs. "We've already discussed the possibility of Master Donnegan's answers being copied from somewhere?"

"He and I were the only people in the Classics Library, Headmaster."

"But 97%? It's virtually unheard of to get such marks."

"The boy obviously possesses an affinity for languages."

"Did you visit the lavatory, Mr Stubbs? Take a tea break?"

"Naturally, Headmaster, but I took care to lock the door and…"

"… It doesn't take long to copy answers concealed in an inside pocket."

"I wasn't away for more than…"

"…You, Mr Stubbs, left this boy to his own resources in the Classics Library, of all places. Surrounded by enough Greek textbooks to sink a ship, eh?" Mr Hoskins picked a crumb off the tip of his tongue. "A quick oral test will eradicate the possibility of any skulduggery."

They think I've cheated!

Mr Hoskins addressed Shane. "St Columbanus is one of the few schools in the West of Ireland teaching Ancient Greek. Your written standard means you'll be well able to understand it. As you know, Homer wrote the world's first storybook, so…" He leant back in his chair and spoke slowly in Ancient Greek, hesitating as he felt for the words. "Tell me something about Homer's tale."

Realising that he understood the Head's every word, Shane wanted to shout that he was freaked out about the whole thing but he commanded himself to breathe deeply. "Homer was blind," he began falteringly in Ancient Greek. "He wrote about the Trojan War and the wanderings of Odysseus, the sacker of cities…"

Wide-eyed, Mr Hoskins raised a hand. "Sacker of cities," he said, turning to the Classics master. "Splendid. Please continue."

Aware that he was speaking faultless Ancient Greek, Shane felt his words were being delivered by someone other than himself, while he listened from somewhere high above his body. "Odysseus," he plunged on with increasing confidence, "took many years to return home from Troy. He was shipwrecked, he met one-eyed giants."

The Headmaster filled a glass from the water decanter and drank quickly. "That will do, Shane," he said softly. "Remarkable. So authentic. I present you with the Scroll of Commendation for exceptional achievement. Sacker of cities, well."

Shane shuffled forward to accept the cardboard tube. "Er, thanks, sir."

"Headmaster, how did Master Donnegan lose those marks?"

"Silly grammatical mistakes. Nonetheless, he still would not have achieved one hundred percent."

Shane cut in, using what he hoped was a respectful tone. "And why's that, sir?"

The Headmaster stood up. The meeting was over. He strode primly across the room and opened the door before replying. "No one gets full marks, otherwise there would be no room for improvement. We must all have room for improvement, staff and pupils alike. Shane, you may regard the coming weeks as your apprenticeship here; I look forward to you joining us next term. Goodbye."

In the main corridor, Shane allowed his puffed out cheeks to deflate as Tubs came running.

"How did it go in the Rat Hole?" Tubs demanded.

"Just the usual blah, blah, blah," Shane began, theatrically slicing the air, using his cardboard tube as a sword. "Hoskins isn't the chirpiest man on the planet, is he? He asked what books I'd read, then I mentioned I was into swimming and straightaway he put my name down for the Sports Day race; and for some field trip... what's that about, Tubs?"

"St Columbanus is twinned with Dublin's Sandymount High School; we do expeditions together; this year's field trip is right here, called, *Westport − Before & After St Patrick*."

"Boring, boring history."

"The Dublin lot stay here in St Columbanus with the boarders. The rest of us crash out in the holiday chalets on Westport Quay." Tubs elbowed Shane and demanded, *"Did you pass the exam?"*

"Yeah, but only after Hoskins made me do an oral in Ancient Greek."

Tubs emitted his distinctive high-pitched laugh. *"Greek?"*

"I was able to tell him about a poet called Homer."

Tubs was ready to guffaw again but stopped. From their flummoxed expressions it was obvious each was as bewildered as the other.

"Homer?" said Tubs.

"Until today, the only Homer I knew was Homer Simpson." Shane glanced around uneasily. "Maybe it's those dreams?"

"What dreams?"

"Weird geezers in strange clothes gabbling away in what I now think was Ancient Greek. Maybe I picked up their lingo in my sleep because all the right stuff just flowed sweetly onto my exam paper."

"Crap," said Tubs, rubbing his cheek. "Maybe it's that BMS stuff?"

"Bee-em-ess?"

"Buried Memory Syndrome."

Shane regarded his friend in silence. *Tubs must eat books for breakfast; he seems to know something about everything. Especially things with big names.*

"They say," continued Tubs, "that chunks of your memory can get passed down from your great-grandfather's brain to yours."

"Come on!"

"Honest. On the news recently, some guy arrived in a town he'd never been to before – yet he knew where the old blacksmith's forge used to be."

"No relation of mine spoke Greek. Granddad lived in Mayo and was a soldier like his brother, Uncle Lionel. Mam's dad was a farmer, left school at fourteen; he could just about speak English, never mind Greek. So pull the other one."

"How do you explain it then, Einstein?"

"Maybe you're right," said Shane, not sounding at all convinced. "Let's say nothing to nobody about this, OK?"

Fighting the urge to point out Shane's grammatical mistake, Tubs handed him a triangle of Toblerone. "Come on, you're going to show me around Clew Bay Lodge…"

"… Sometimes, Tubs, I wonder who I really am."

Chapter 4

"Take your mark – GO!"

Sports Day's 100-metre open race was the final event and St Columbus' all-glass swimming complex was crammed. As the five other swimmers plunged into the pool with practised ease, Shane, the sixth competitor, had faltered on his starting block.

A shout came from the audience. "You couldn't win a raffle, Donkey Dung, never mind win a race."

They all think I'm a joke. I'll show them...

Before he hit the water, Shane saw odds-on favourite, Jeremy Brockenhurst, was already in the lead.

His furious initial strokes propelled him past the two stragglers battling to avoid coming last and within seconds only two metres separated him from Frank Preston and Nick Mahon who were slogging it out for second place. On reaching the halfway mark and as the shouting grew louder, he slammed the soles of his feet against the tiles and accelerated into the final straight, leaving Mahon and Preston behind. Oblivious to Shane's late challenge, the smirk on Brockenhurst's face become more pronounced as almost neck and neck, both swimmers powered towards the finish. Brockenhurst was still cocksure the race was his. Despite their age difference, Shane was gaining and seeing the smug amazement on the leader's face turn to rage, he dodged Brockenhurst's attempt to strike him as he passed in the inside lane.

Tubs' warning was spot on – Brockenhurst always has a dirty trick up his sleeve.

Shane's hand thudded against the tiles; he had taken the race by almost two metres. Sucking throbbing knuckles, he pulled off his goggles to survey the sea of incredulous expressions. Brockenhurst's face was a similar mask of disbelief.

"SILENCE!"

The headmaster's bark over the loudspeaker quelled the shouts and catcalls from the audience. He drummed his fingers on the balcony until the last murmur died away. "St Columbanus proudly announces the result of the freestyle race…"

He stopped speaking as the PE teacher, Mr Kavanagh, handed him a computer printout which he quickly read. "It appears that Master Donnegan also broke the school record… remarkable for a fourteen-year-old."

Using any old excuse to let rip, some pupils began foot stamping. Shane Donnegan, a total unknown, breaking swimming records?

No one expected me to win the race. I was only squeezed in at the last minute. I'm not even breathing hard…

Shane wished his glowing face would cool as he shuffled onto the winner's podium, hoping that his inner bewilderment wasn't obvious. As Mr Kavanagh draped the winner's ribbon over his shoulders, Tubs laughingly called out, "Shane, you swam like your bum was on fire."

"Less of that talk, McAuley," snapped Mr Kavanagh.

"Sorry, sir."

Mr Kavanagh said, "Shane, I only slotted you in because you're big for your age. You did a lot of swimming in Australia, yes?"

Shane smiled self-consciously. "Just my lucky day, sir."

"There was nothing *lucky* about that swim. You'd be a dead cert to win an All-Ireland medal in your age group – given the right amount of hard work."

"Hard work?" said Shane, his eyes narrowing.

"Winning such an honour would naturally involve regular gym sessions, daily runs in the sand dunes plus the usual pool routines. And, of course, evening classes in sport science theory..."

"... Sounds *really* great, sir," interrupted Shane.

If he heard the irony, the teacher ignored it and plunged on. "You could stay over in school each weekend getting into shape and..."

"... Nice thought, sir, and thanks, but karate's my thing, not swimming."

"But surely your parents would love to have a swimming champion in the family?"

"Mam's dead, sir," said Shane matter-of-factly, "and Dad's in Oz." *All-Ireland medal or no All-Ireland medal, nothing is going to interfere with my time off.* "But, tell you what, sir?"

"Uh, huh?"

"With a bit more practice," he said unconvincingly, "I might knock another bit off that record, yeah?"

Realising he'd lost the battle – getting Shane Donnegan to do any extra work would obviously be a minor miracle – Mr Kavanagh shot him a knowing look. "Well done, anyway" he sighed.

"Thanks, sir."

As the two friends made their way to the changing rooms, Shane's voice dropped. "No way, Tubs, am I sloshing around in smelly chlorine just to win medals."

"Fess up, Shane," said Tubs, coming to a standstill. "How did you win that race?"

Each saw the same perplexed expression on the other's face.

"I just went for it, Tubs."

Still brimming with questions, they sauntered

towards the swing doors of the changing rooms.

"Oi, Donkey Dung." It was Jeremy Brockenhurst, blocking the entrance, a towel around his shoulders.

"Lost something, Jeremy?" said Shane innocently.

Brockenhurst's fists were clenching and unclenching. "I would've taken freestyle three years running if it wasn't for you, you cheat."

Shane's nostrils flared. "What did you call me?" he said, dropping into a slightly crouched position.

Brockenhurst's lip curled. "Your ears are full of koala snot. You must be on steroids, or pep pills."

Shane felt a twinge of empathy, appreciating what losing such a race must've meant to someone who spent more hours in the pool than the rest of the senior team put together. "Winning prizes isn't my thing," he muttered. "I was only squeezed in because two finalists were laid up."

"That's the truth, Jeremy," pleaded Tubs.

Deciding to make a final stab at keeping the peace, Shane added, "You take the medal if it's that important to you; I'll tell Hoskins I'm just not bothered."

Brockenhurst's face had a baffled look. "You don't hand back medals, Donkey Dung," he grunted. As he slouched into the changing rooms, he called over his shoulder, "Watch your step, sunshine."

"Forget Brockenhurst, Shane," said Tubs, "the Sandymount High School bus is outside."

"Whoever heard of going on a field trip in your hometown?"

"I like history trips."

"Speak for yourself."

Chapter 5

Shane looked around the table. "Something stinks about Westport House," he said, a challenge in his eyes.

The school bus had been delayed so Shane, Tubs, Caveman and Scruffy were hogging the window seats of *The Helm Cafe.* Situated at Westport Quay on the banks of the Carrowbeg River, the popular spot made the ideal meeting-place for the field-trippers and despite being situated outside Westport town, it was always heaving. Zara was making her way to their table.

"Hey, why is Lady Muck coming to join *us?*" grated Caveman through the corner of his mouth.

Shane whispered, "The others in her group are down with some bug or other so Stubbs squeezed her in." Moving his chair to make extra room, he said brightly, "Hi, Zara, I was just saying there's something weird about Westport House."

"Like what?" said Tubs, wiping crumbs from his lips. He had to raise his voice because the place was buzzing as the other pupils yakked and horsed around, joking and laughing the time away. A table tennis table and a pool table stood in the adjoining annexe where an ancient jukebox, flashing psychedelic lighting, drowned out the clatter and clunk of balls.

Shane held up a copy of the *Mayo News.* "That's two drownings there since Lord Dunraven bought Westport House. I checked out the latest victim on Facebook; he's the County's surfing champ, looks like Mr Universe. I say we pop in for a quick squizz around that new industrial park Dunraven's built."

Caveman flexed his wide shoulders. "People are always drowning," he grunted. "That's life."

"Shane's right," Zara said, displaying her Mona

35

Lisa smile. "Last week Dunraven closed Westport House to the public. OK, so he's made our field trip an exception – for *educational reasons* – but we'll be the last ones allowed on the Estate. Ever."

Shane threw her a quizzical look. *Support from Her Majesty? I was expecting another dirty look...*

"I've checked out Dunraven on Google, TikTok and Instagram," said Scruffy, straightening a crease in his trousers. "Making cleaning stuff is hardly worth drowning people for, in my humble opinion."

Shane smiled. Peter really did care about his clothes, even knowing what colours went with what. Tubs had nicknamed him Scruffy. "So why all the heavy security?" continued Shane. "His buildings remind me of a prisoner of war camp; all that's missing are…"

"… Torture chambers," sniped Tubs, giving his high-pitched squeal.

Zara cupped her face in her hands. "Maybe Dunraven has an allergy?"

"To burglars?" said Caveman.

"Very funny," said Zara.

"Mrs Durcan reckons Dunraven's dodgy," said Shane.

"Who's Mrs Durcan?" demanded Scruffy.

"She looks after the holiday chalets; she says Dunraven wouldn't lower himself to chat to any of the locals."

A humorous drawl cut in. "Idle talk from idle layabouts." It was *The Helm's* owner, Vinny Keogh, coming from the kitchen, trademark dishcloth slung over his shoulder. For some reason he'd taken to Shane's group and enjoyed shooting the breeze with them. Tubs had immediately christened him Dishcloth.

"Now, children," Dishcloth continued, "when I

was a youngster, I thought Dracula lived in Westport House and..."

"... Weren't you always a bit of a dreamer, Dishcloth?" cut in Shane.

Dishcloth lifted a pastry from the confectionery rack then zoomed it playfully at Shane, who deftly netted the bun with his outstretched cap. Lifting it out, he pretended to nibble. "Yum-yum; any chance of the recipe?"

Dishcloth plunged on as if nothing had happened. "Shane has a point. I do maintenance and lunch stuff for Dunraven's new complex; he warns me not to hang around – for my own good, he says."

Scruffy nodded. "Just like my old man when I help clean up our hotel; and the slave driver only pays me eight euros an hour."

"Eight euros?" spluttered Caveman. "My Dad would kill me if I didn't help out around the farm. And I don't get a penny."

Shane grinned; anyone in St Columbanus attempting to land a blow on Caveman, the Fifth Class' biggest and tallest, would be taking a particularly risky gamble.

"Aside from the gatekeepers," continued Dishcloth, "Dunraven has security brutes everywhere; they say nothing, just stare at you like psychos."

Shane felt his curiosity increase. "What's this Dunraven like?"

"Snotty English accent; swanky suits; as friendly as a tractor," said Dishcloth.

"But what does he *do* in the factory?" insisted Scruffy. "Apart from making dosh?"

"He's some sort of a doctor."

"Witch doctor," sniggered Tubs.

"Papa says Dunraven was once a surgeon in

India," said Zara.

"See?" said Shane rapping the table. "Nothing adds up. I say we jump the walls; check out what's really going on."

"Now listen here, Donnegan-from-Down-Under," said Dishcloth firmly. "Nobody *sensible* goes within a mile of that place; it's not your average suburban bungalow." Realising he had everyone's attention, his voice dropped. "At midnight, Dunraven releases two starving Dobermanns to patrol the Estate; they've eaten every wild animal around, there's hardly a rabbit left." He added in a doom-laden undertone, "Their yowling would scare the living daylights out of you."

Shane felt as if he'd been doused with iced water. But Dishcloth wasn't finished. "Last summer I watched those weirdo guards push laden wheelbarrows through the gardens…"

"… Laden with what?" interrupted Caveman with customary bullishness.

"Looked like raw meat."

"Maybe he has a small private zoo?" suggested Zara. "Sort of hobby a rich guy might have; the Estate is more than big enough."

"Free advice, Dunraven's place is strictly no-go." Dishcloth made a slicing motion across his throat.

You can never be sure with Dishcloth; he gets a kick out of scaring us with his way-out stories...

"A few pooches, Dishcloth!" came a sneering voice from nearby. It was Jeremy Brockenhurst, leaning back on his chair, heels on the table. "Come off it! I wouldn't be scared to check out what's going on – and I bet it's not much."

Dishcloth ignored Brockenhurst's outburst and returning to the kitchen, called over his shoulder, "Don't say you haven't been warned, Shane."

Brockenhurst thumped the table and backed by his Wolf Pack – the Delahunt twins, Kev and Hopalong – the three began to holler:

> *Donkey Dung Donnegan's*
> *A snotty little mouse.*
> *He hasn't got the balls to climb*
> *The walls of Westport House.*

Dishcloth silenced the outburst by surging through the kitchen doors, waving a cloth above his head. "Cut out that racket, Brockenhurst," he thundered, "or I'll personally sort you out." His tone suggested it would be a bad idea to disobey.

"Me? Moi?" Brockenhurst whined, playing the injured innocent but backtracking nonetheless for the exit. "Remember, Donkey Dung, if anyone's going over Dunraven's walls, it certainly won't be *you*."

Chapter 6

"Don't let that missing link bug you, Shane," Zara said as Brockenhurst departed.

"Pot Hole can't resist showin' off in front of the girls."

"Those Dobermanns *are* a problem," Shane conceded. "But – I've got a plan." As he gestured the others closer, a shout came from the main entrance.

"Donnegan!" Mr Stubbs was holding the main door ajar and pointing outside. "The bus is leaving."

From the rear seat, Shane watched the sea and distant Clare Island disappear from view as Mr Stubbs, standing beside the driver, addressed the packed bus. "Our first stop today is Westport House itself, where Professor Henry Hughes will lead our tour and take the scholarship class. The rest of you will be divided between myself and the other guides. I expect proper manners and no smarty-pants questions."

As the bus passed through the entry gates of the Westport House Estate, Shane saw a heron rise and flap awkwardly from its fishing spot on the Carrowbeg river. He leaned backwards trying to see what had disturbed the bird, following its ponderous flight until it was lost in the sun's glare. *Wish I was as patient as those herons... wonder what my old mates back in Brisbane High would say if they could see me now...*

The bus braked without warning. Splayed across the road lay the tangled branches of two fallen oak trees that had crashed through the outer wall of the Estate.

"Some storm last night," said the driver, manoeuvring around the twisted mass. "It'll be next week before that wall's repaired."

With their horizontal trunks stretching some

distance beyond the shattered boundary and their roots splayed at weird angles, the fallen trees reminded Shane of the outstretched fingers of some incredible giant. *You could get a Centurion tank through that hole in the wall… that storm's done us a big favour…*

As they approached the waterfall, Shane caught his first glimpse of Westport House through the roadside trees. The majestic limestone structure stood on a slight elevation, its imposing grey colouration standing out in stark contrast to the surrounding greenery and sweeping woodland. On leaping from the bus outside the House, Shane tried to link arms with Tubs.

"Get lost, Shane. No way am I facin' savage dogs."

Shane nodded understandingly. "Yeah, the dogs could be a problem, but…" he waved Scruffy and Tubs a little closer, "… I've got the answer."

Before Shane could explain, Mr Stubbs' voice cut in. "Finbar McAuley, you go with Professor Hughes. The rest of you, follow me; remember, bonus marks for diagrams and original ideas."

Shane whispered against the back of his hand, "Remember, we link up at Mrs Durcan's at half-eight; her chalet is the last one on the holiday block."

***

Shane was still writing, two open textbooks at his elbow. Loose sheets of paper and crumpled pages lay scattered across the chalet table, all covered in his distinctive electrocardiogram scrawl. He didn't look up as Tubs poked his head around the door.

"Writin'?" Tubs said. "What's wrong with your laptop?"

Shane frowned, somehow feeling embarrassed, as if he'd been caught doing something disreputable. "It's my report for tomorrow and I prefer using a pen. Is that a crime?"

"You doin' *extra* work? I thought you were allergic to history?"

"It's just that…" Shane stared sightlessly at the plaster flight of green ducks ascending the chalet wall, "… the tour of the Estate was awesome."

"Did you go around with Stubbs?"

"No, with one of the guides. Just me and him; the muscly guy with the beard."

Tubs frowned as he unwrapped a toffee. "I saw nobody like that."

"He just came up to me, said he was an official guide and that he recognised my ring."

"Your mum's ring, you mean?"

"He called himself Don; he really knew his stuff. He explained what the signs on the boulders were and that sort of thing. I sort of felt as if…" He fell silent.

"*As if* what"?"

"As if I'd been there before…"

"Like when you were a leprechaun?" chortled Tubs. "Maybe you were there to help Grace O'Malley – *Gráinne Ní Mháile* to you – build her castle, eh?"

"Yeah, yeah, yeah – she was Ireland's Pirate Queen and she used the same Westport House site to build her castle here in the 16th century – blah-di-blah-di-blah. I reckon the original foundations of Westport House go back thousands of years."

"*You* reckon?" hooted Tubs, making no attempt to conceal his incredulity. "If Prof Hughes says that Westport House was built in fifteen-whenever, then that's it, pal. What other headbanger's stuff did that guide feed you, yeah? And how come we never saw him?"

Shane bit his lip. *How come nobody else saw my guide? Strange, if it's true...* "A funny thing happened when I met him..." He fell silent as if he was unsure of what to say or how to say it.

"What?"

"My, er, ring began to shine; a purple colour..."

"... It's what happens when sunlight reflects off rings, you clown."

"I suppose you're right."

Shane became aware of the TV blaring from Mrs Durcan's next door. As she shrieked in unison with the canned laughter on some American sitcom, he didn't hear Zara enter the kitchen, Caveman and Scruffy in tow.

"We're going to be first over those walls," she began, hands on her hips. "Brockenhurst won't make fools of us again in front of everyone. By the way, Papa told me Brockenhurst was kicked out of Eton."

Hey, she's actually on my side!

"Eating what?" said Caveman.

"Ha, ha, ha," said Zara sarcastically.

"Eton's the poshest school in England," said Scruffy, clapping Caveman's shoulder.

"Does Brockenhurst still wear that sweatshirt with the wolves on the back?" said Tubs.

"Not wolves," said Caveman. "Deer."

Tubs' shoulders shook. "Wolves – I should know," he chortled. "I drew sunglasses on them when he was in the pool."

"I want to hear about Shane's *Big Entry Plan,*" said Zara.

"It's simple, Zara," said Shane. "We pop through the smashed wall and explore for an hour. Dishcloth is positive the Dobermanns are never released before midnight."

As the others began to jabber at once, Scruffy said, "In my opinion, that's no plan at all."

"What if Dunraven releases the dogs early?" said Tubs, nibbling his nails.

Mischief danced in Shane's eyes. "I'll put them to sleep."

"Sing them lullabies?" snorted Caveman.

"No, feed them meat with sleeping tablets."

"Sleeping tablets!" chorused Tubs and Scruffy, looking at Shane as if he'd morphed into a vampire.

"Listen," said Shane, reverting to full persuasive mode. "Since her husband died, Mrs Durcan just watches TV and talks about how grand things were when she was a girl. Yesterday she slipped me ten euros to clear out her hubby's room – clothes, old medicines and that – all he ever took were sleeping tablets and cod liver oil." He tapped his backpack. "Mr Durcan's pills are either for the Dobermanns' supper or the dustbin. Decide."

I won't bore them with that sad stuff about her hip replacement and gall bladder removal or how her husband laid Dunraven's sewage system... I felt really so sorry for her; hope I die before I get that old...

Scruffy's indignant voice cut through his thoughts. "No way am I getting involved in drugs..."

"... Me neither," snapped Shane. "This is a one-off. If those Dobermanns turn up – and that's a big if – we toss them beef chunks mixed with Mr Durcan's tablets."

"Sleeping tablets are dangerous," said Scruffy, his voice rising. "And maybe they won't work."

"Why shouldn't they work?" snapped Shane.

"They might be past their BBD," said Tubs.

"What's bee-bee-dee?" grunted Caveman.

45

"Best before date," sighed Zara, looking heavenwards.

"The label says they're still OK," said Shane.

Zara squeezed Shane's hand under the tablecloth. "It sounds very iffy," she whispered.

"Far too dodgy," added Scruffy emphatically.

"I'm on board," said Caveman, cracking his knuckles.

Shane addressed Tubs and Scruffy. "Come on, you two," he enthused, "we'll be in and out in twenty minutes flat."

Both looked as if they were suffering from severe constipation.

Shane flashed his mega-watt smile. "If we all agree then we go in… tonight!"

"I'd rather drink battery acid," said Scruffy.

Shane's intent gaze switched from one face to another. "Let's find out what's what. It may be nothing but at least we'll blow Brockenhurst's reputation sky-high by getting in first." *I reckon Caveman and Scruffy are with me; Miss Singh and Tubs are a different matter...* "Zara," he continued earnestly, "maybe Dunraven is doing animal experiments?"

"Injecting shampoo into rabbits' ears?" she said, her eyes misting.

"And then what?" demanded Tubs. "Complain to the Society For Bullied Bunnies? Anyway, we're grounded after lights out."

Shane took a deep breath. "Stubbs always conks out early and Mrs Durcan is already on the sherry. She'll snore like a train in front of the screen; you'd need a grenade to waken her." He thumped the table. "Let's vote – who's for exploring?"

Four hands rose.

"Scared, Tubs?" said Caveman bullishly.

Tubs threw him a look that would've frozen hot chocolate. "If it's all the same to you, Hercules, I'm behind with my report; I've only written twenty-five pages."

"Twenty-five!" cried Scruffy.

"In or out?" demanded Caveman.

Tubs didn't reply. Aware he was the centre of attention, he milked it for a while longer before slowly raising his hand. "Can we take Snoog?" he asked meekly.

Hearing its name mentioned, Snoog appeared from beneath the table, its tail thumping against the bench – Mrs Durcan's small mongrel had taken a real shine to Tubs and would follow him anywhere. Because he knew nothing would interfere with Tubs' studies, Mr Stubbs had turned a blind eye, provided the dog was kept on a leash.

Tubs patted Snoog's head. "Mrs Durcan claims he's a good guard dog… "

"… Against houseflies," scoffed Caveman.

"Snoog can come," said Shane, "provided Tubs keeps him quiet." He punched the air. "Dunraven, here we come."

Chapter 7

The night was fresh and breezy, cloaked with fast-moving cloud and intermittent moonlight. Only creaking branches and the rustlings of small night creatures broke the woodland silence.

"It feels as if the human race has been wiped out," whispered Shane into Zara's ear as they hunched beneath the high walls of Westport House Estate. *Everything seems taller and spookier than in the daylight. These huge tree trunks remind me of those forest spirits from my old Grimm's storybook...*

A line of stone griffins stared down at him, their crouched heads wreathed in foliage from the vegetation that grew inside the Estate and overhung the walls. Rows of barbed wire were angled outwards to prevent would-be intruders from throwing coats or sacks to neutralise the spikes. The branches of the toppled oaks had been chain sawed away and two lines of rope stretched across the gaping hole on which a sign hung:

GUARD DOGS – NO ENTRY
DO NOT EVEN <u>THINK</u> ABOUT IT

"Someone doesn't like tourists," muttered Tubs.

"Switch off phones; follow me," grated Shane, clambering along the horizontal trunk. He was surprised at the smallness of his voice.

Why on earth did I get involved in this? It's one thing getting riled by Brockenhurst; it's a different ballgame up here in the dark. His torchlight illuminated their pale faces.

"Those dogs will see us!" squealed Tubs.

"Don't wet yourself," said Caveman. "They're

not due for hours yet."

"Keep quiet," snapped Shane, taking Snoog under his arm.

Using the sawn-off stumps as handgrips, they scrambled upwards and tottered along the uneven surface until reaching the Keep Out sign. As Shane lifted the ropes to allow the others to clamber through, a loud ringing above their heads shattered the silence.

"Oh, my God," said Zara, pointing to the line of dancing security bells that were making the almighty racket on the ropes.

"They'll wake the dead," gasped Tubs.

As the jangling peaked then subsided, Snoog growled.

"What's *that*?" croaked Scruffy.

No answer was required. The fusillade of distant barking chilled Shane's blood as they stared at each other with widening eyes. "The Dobermanns," he whispered.

Tubs grabbed Shane's arm. "Let's get out quick."

"Before it's too late," added Zara.

"Time for Plan B," said Shane, intending his voice to sound confident but it came out more like a rasp.

"Roll on the mongrels," said Caveman calmly.

"How many tablets in each chunk?" cried Tubs.

"Four," said Shane as calmly as he could, even though his knees were threatening to fold.

"Those things sound like hungry wolves," hissed Scruffy.

"The tablets will knock out a full-grown rhino," said Shane. He hoped that sounded good, it was the sort of thing he heard heroes say on Netflix, but a feeling of dread was working down his insides like concentrated acid.

"The vet's surgery where I work Saturdays," said

Zara fiercely, "uses the same red tablets to put sick animals to sleep."

Shane emptied small plastic bags of meat from his backpack. "Zara, Tubs and Scruffy throw handfuls to the left," he said, aware that Snoog's teeth were bared. "Caveman and me, to the right. Then we sit still and wait."

And hope.

He could hear the dogs crashing headlong through the undergrowth. No barks this time, just deep-throated growls. Like torpedoes with teeth, they burst into the open, streaking across the clearing, heading unerringly in great bounds towards the fallen oaks, moonlight glinting in their wild eyes.

"They're the size of... of... donkeys," stammered Zara.

Thirty metres from the fallen oaks, the dogs came to a standstill, furiously sniffing the ground. Temporarily losing interest in the intruders, they attacked the scattered meat, downing the pieces quickly; sometimes tossing the portions into the air before swallowing them whole, their snapping jaws sounding abnormally loud in the woodland silence. Having gulped down the last morsel, both animals refocused on the trees, their hunger obviously far from sated.

"The tablets aren't strong enough," croaked Tubs, trying to shield himself behind Shane.

As the smaller Dobermann moved forward, he looked around at its companion, a slightly dazed expression settling over its features. Almost in slow motion, it looked up into the night before refocusing on something ahead. Bending to sniff the ground, its knees began to buckle and with eyelids flickering, it keeled over with what sounded to Shane like a contented sigh. Almost mimicking its companion, the larger dog's forelegs began to trip over themselves and it likewise rolled over soundlessly in a heap.

Shane leapt to the ground and prodded each prostrate animal with the toe of his trainers. "We did it," he whispered, releasing his pent-up breath.

"Yee-hee," came Tubs' hysterical laugh as he wiped his palms on his jeans.

"That's the easy bit," said Shane.

With every nerve as taut as overstretched guitar strings, he waved the others on, ready to duck into denser foliage at the slightest sign of danger. Despite the coolness of the night air, his clothes felt clammy against his back.

"It's pitch dark," whispered Tubs. "How come you can see, Shane?

"I was just thinking the same," muttered Zara.

Shane froze. A red dot had glowed, then disappeared – forty metres away. Heart thumping, he remained motionless.

"What is it?" whispered Caveman.

"Somebody smoking. Near that hut. Stay here." Shane crawled forwards, sweat running into his eyes, dust flecking his lips. Remaining in the shadows, he crept as close as he dared to the small cabin before propping himself against the metal structure. The voices told him two men were inside.

"*...And I hope the Dobermanns eat the backsides off them dozy locals, Pete.*"

"*Shouldn't we check?*"

"*Nah, those dogs will have seen them off. Only four of Schwartz's mob on duty tonight. Big consignment coming up. Dunraven's zombies give me the spooks. I'm for watchin' that Netflix film...*"

"...Keep the volume down, Rob; I need me beauty sleep."

"Take a lot of sleep to make you beautiful, Pete."

With the guards' guffaws ringing in his ears, Shane retreated.

After recounting to the others what he'd overheard, he added, "There's only four guards on duty so let's explore that building over there; it should only take a few minutes."

"Who did they mean, *zombies*?" whispered Scruffy.

"Those psycho brutes Dishcloth spoke about," said Shane.

"How long will those hounds be sleepin' for?"

"Couple of hours. We'll be well in bed by then." *I hope....*

Chapter 8

In single file they moved into the sloping field close to where the long metallic building lay, vibrating with a faint hum. As they moved downhill, Shane squinted at the lines of tall poles, each suspending large fronds of strangely-shaped plants, hairy and festooned with curious flowers. They reminded him of massively-oversized runner beans with unpleasant, bulging pods. Snoog was excitedly sniffing the ground.

"Phew," said Scruffy, holding his nose.

"They stink of rotten meat," whispered Zara.

"Or Caveman's socks," spluttered Tubs.

Shane ducked low. "Someone's coming."

They whipped back into the shadows as two flash-light beams swept the garden, some seventy metres away, followed by the sound of approaching footsteps. Then came a very familiar voice.

"Keep your voices down, you pair of tossers."

There was no mistaking who it was – Brockenhurst and his Wolf Pack!

Shane froze as an ominous growl came from the bushes close to where he crouched – a large animal was nosing through the undergrowth, heading in his direction.

"Here, boy," came Brockenhurst's soft call but the menace in his voice was unmistakable.

Brockenhurst has his dog in tow! So have we, mind. Not that Snoog would be much use in a fight...

The inquisitive animal, its colour almost indistinguishable from the surrounding shadows, had obviously picked up Shane's track but it reluctantly traipsed back towards its master, a disgruntled growl lingering in its throat.

Shane heard Brockenhurst drive his fist into the

animal's ribcage, grunting with each consecutive word. "Come – when – you're – called – boy." Releasing the whimpering dog, Brockenhurst grated, "Kev, where the hell are you?"

"Over here, with Hopalong."

As Snoog cowered between his legs, Shane hardly dared blink, while the Delahunt twins, illuminated by a sudden shaft of torchlight, scurried forward like twitchy animals.

Brockenhurst laughed. "I just knew Donnegan and his fairies wouldn't have the guts. Let's see if there's anything worth nicking."

"What's that awful stink, J?"

Brockenhurst's German Shepherd was also agitated by the pungent odour. On its hind legs, the dog began sniffing one of the plants, forepaws resting on the pole, exploring the long stem. As the animal's nose came into contact with the pod's exterior, the entire shell shot open, exposing a bright pink interior. Simultaneously, long white tentacles darted outwards, wrenched the mesmerised animal off its feet and whipped it inside.

A vertical column of long spikes protruded from the internal surfaces of the pod and the shell closed around the animal, its shuddering body becoming quickly transfixed. The whole incident had taken less than six seconds.

Kev's voice was almost inaudible. "Did you see *that…?*"

"Those spikes must be poisoned…" croaked Brockenhurst. "Let's get the hell outta here."

Eyes fixated on the plants, the three Wolf Packers reversed at speed into the darkness. Only the widening dark stain on the earth beneath the pod showed that something very strange had taken place.

Chapter 9

Nobody moved until the Wolf Pack had long been swallowed by the night. One apprehensive step at a time, Shane exited the vegetable plot, Snoog in his arms, every cell in his body on maximum alert. Each shadow now seemed laden with threats of fresh dangers, every breath of wind sounded like approaching guards. Or worse.

"This field is full of those... things," said Zara, shielding her mouth and nose.

Scruffy's eyes darted from side to side. "I'm for out-of-here. Now."

"Shane, let's get back," pleaded Tubs.

I mustn't let them know I'm just as freaked out as they are... "Those things are some sort of giant Venus fly traps," he said, shaking his head, trying to dismiss the memory. "They're unreal."

"Ask that dog if they're unreal," growled Caveman.

"Those wheelbarrows Dishcloth mentioned," said Zara, "maybe it was meat to feed those things? No way can they be normal plants."

"Genetically modified," said Tubs matter-of-factly.

"Why change small plants into giant meat eaters?" muttered Caveman.

"It doesn't make sense," whispered Scruffy. "Dunraven wouldn't make any profit..."

"Ssh! Someone's coming," cut in Shane.

In the distance, two flashlight beams were sweeping the long field, moving in their direction. Silhouettes of two men appeared against the skyline. Stopping to light cigarettes, their conversation became audible.

"...I'm telling ye, Pete, I saw three yobbos scurry

57

through the wall."

"They must've poisoned the Dobermanns... maybe we shouldn't put it in our report?"

"Everything goes into that report, Pete; he's got eyes in the back of his head."

"Let's double check that no others stayed behind."

As the guards advanced, Shane, a finger across his lips, pointed at the long outhouse lying outside the gardens. "Quick! There's nowhere else to hide."

Resembling a squat aircraft hangar, the building showed neither windows nor lights.

The four followed Shane along the dark pathway, keeping a wide berth between themselves and the plants. They scrambled around the side of the featureless building, desperately seeking a way to get inside but there was none; only smooth metal met their desperate eyes and fingers. Finally reaching the rear, they were confronted by a featureless aluminium door.

"Damn," gasped Caveman, fumbling around in the darkness. "Where's the latch?" Finding no handle, only a slim metal keypad, he drove his shoulder against the unyielding door.

The guards' flashlights were sweeping the grounds less than seventy metres away when Zara pushed Caveman aside. "You couldn't change a light bulb; let Tubs try."

Tubs pulled a console from his backpack and flicked on the small screen. "This little beaut is my own invention," he muttered, confidently pressing buttons. "It can change TV channels, break circuits and that sort of thing. Basically it's your bog standard hand-held; added memory, Wi-Fi attachments and…"

"…Hurry, Tubs," grated Zara. "They're almost on top of us."

Shane watched a tiny light oscillate above the lock, followed by a metallic hiss. How they all managed to stumble inside before the door noiselessly closed behind them, he'd never know.

Inside the confined, square-shaped hallway, Shane waited for the guards' footfalls to fade before sizing up the strange, metallic surroundings. The dark-red glow that pulsated throughout the building intensified the lines on their faces. Lab coats hung from wall racks, rows of white wellingtons sat on the floor, squat electronic junction boxes lined the walls. Dead ahead, another metallic door led into the building itself.

"Infrared lightin'; some kind of changin' room…" began Tubs.

"…We're not *totally* blind, Finbar," said Zara.

"Let's have a quick scout around," whispered Shane.

The large bronze plaque above the entrance read:

PHASE 1
BIOLOGICAL PREPARATION
AUTHORISED PERSONNEL ONLY

Scruffy caught Shane's arm. "Trespassing is a criminal offence, in case you didn't know."

"Let's see what's going on behind that door, OK?" Without waiting for an answer, Shane propelled Tubs towards the entrance. "Do your stuff, chief engineer," he whispered.

"Same code as outside, Shane."

As the door hissed open, all followed Shane into the long, factory-like structure, their eyes slowly adjusting to the eerie lighting. As they progressed through each consecutive section, overhead fluorescents came on to illuminate the way, automatically extinguishing as the group of friends moved on.

It feels as if the building is alive, anticipating our every step...

Ahead, a row of six metallic drums, each five metres high, met his gaze. A metal ladder ran up the side of each container, which were fed from above by a series of inter-connecting tanks. Pressure gauges, keypads and dials of various sizes lined the adjacent walls. Electric cables, as thick as a man's wrist, snaked across the roof, running up the sides of the building and along the floor. Everywhere resonated with a powerful electronic hum.

Shane placed his palm on the nearest cauldron. "Something's cooking inside."

"Irish stew?" said Caveman.

"You're hilarious," snapped Zara.

Shane ignored their remarks. "Whatever's in there is being fed into these cooking machines. Tubs, scoot up; check what's inside."

"I'm, er, not that great with heights, Shane…"

"…Outta my way," said Caveman, pushing Tubs aside and clambering up the ladder.

He peered into the vat then stepped back, his white knuckles grasping the rail. "It's full of those meat-eating plants."

Shane muttered, "Why boil down giant Venus fly-traps?"

"In my opinion," said Scruffy, "Dunraven hardly needs guards to protect tubs of vegetable stew, yeah?"

"Let's see where all this stuff ends up. Then home…"

Without warning, multiple ceiling and wall lights illuminated every corner of the building with magnesium-bright light. Green beacons simultaneously flashed on the top of each vat. From hidden speakers, a mechanical voice intoned, *"Boiling and rendering cycle is complete."*

As the vibrating inside the vats subsided, Shane's attention switched to the conveyor belt at the end of the building, which had abruptly clattered into life. All five edged forwards to see empty, litre-sized jars being transported on the belt, then juddering to a halt below the last vat. Through a narrow glass chute, dark pink liquid poured down to fill each passing jar which was automatically sealed and labelled.

"Six seconds, to fill and stamp each jar," announced Tubs.

"What's Dunraven using this stuff for?" said Caveman.

"Something to do with his animal experiments, I bet," whispered Zara.

Shane pointed. "The belt's taking the stuff outside. Come on, let's follow."

As a loud gurgling noise made them instinctively swing around, Tubs pointed. "It's stuff goin' down that wastepipe."

"All that filth goes into the river," said Zara, clenching her fists.

The low growl at his feet made Shane freeze. *Hey, Snoog's not such a bad guard dog after all.* "Hide!" he said, whipping the dog under his arm and pushing Zara and Tubs behind the line of hi-vis jackets. The five squatted low and remained motionless, hypnotically watching the rear door slide noiselessly open.

Two powerfully-built men with closely-cropped hair entered, blue eyes focused ahead. Dressed in boiler suits and white t-shirts, they resembled identical twins. In perfect time and without breaking step, they marched forward like something out of a well-rehearsed film scene.

Shane had stopped breathing. *The zombies!*

"They're comin' straight for us," croaked Tubs.

"Not another word," whispered Shane.

He made a final check that nothing could be viewed through chinks in the intervening line of coats, patted Snoog, sank low and waited.

The men's thick-soled boots made no noise as they strode on like robots, jaws firmly set.

Chapter 10

Snoog cowered in Shane's arms as the two marched past their hiding place without a sideways glance. They halted at the conveyor belt where one consulted his iPad, the other spoke into a walkie-talkie he'd unhooked from the wall.

"Bi-o-log-ical Prep-ar-a-tion," came his guttural voice. A pause, then, "Six bottles per vat. Thirty-six bottles for collection."

He talks like Gustav what's-his-name in the Sixth Class, from Germany...

A well-spoken English voice ended the blare of static. "Are you categorically certain, No 3? I was anticipating a considerably larger volume."

Dunraven!

The guard's flat monotone repeated, "Thirty-six bottles for collection."

"Transportation is on its way," came Dunraven's reply. "Reset then get yourself and No 4 back here to Cryogenics. Tomorrow, I want the harvesting detail increased. More fodder production is required. Out."

Shane saw the two guards nod to each other, replace the walkie-talkie then exit the plant. Immediately the lights extinguished, the ground and ceiling engines simultaneously came to life, suffusing the plant in the same dim lighting as before.

"They hardly spoke to each other," whispered Scruffy.

"Dishcloth was right, they're like zombies," said Shane, whisking the walkie-talkie from the wall and slipping it into his backpack. He winked at Zara, who was watching, a burning question in her eyes. "Just borrowing it," he mouthed.

"They looked like twins," said Tubs.

"They looked seriously mean to me," added Caveman, cracking his knuckles.

"Lots of things look mean to you, Caveman," said Zara before asking Tubs, "What's cryogenics?"

"It means keepin' things frozen," began Tubs.

"I know that, duh, but why would Dunraven need cryogenics?" she insisted.

"Let's find out," said Shane. "Follow those guards."

Scruffy grabbed Shane's arm. "You said this was to be our last stop."

"Please, Scruff, just a few more minutes, then home, right?"

As Tubs completed punching in the exit codes, they saw an electric van pull away from the building, its rear section stacked with crates of juice-filled containers. The driver's appearance was identical to the other guards.

"Stay behind me," Shane whispered, jogging well behind the slow-moving vehicle but keeping in the woodland shadow.

A hundred metres on, the vehicle braked in front of another windowless, metallic building, its entrance illuminated by ground-based searchlights. Three uniformed guards appeared, unloaded the containers and carried them inside without exchanging a word. The van then pulled away, leaving the building in darkness. The whole procedure had taken less than two minutes.

"Notice anything about the guards?" whispered Shane.

Caveman nodded. "They're all spitting images of each other."

Scruffy pushed his Rolex under Shane's nose. "Seen the time?"

"OK, OK, we'll head off now…"

"… But how do we get out, Shane?" interrupted Tubs. "Those security gorillas will be watchin' the hole in the wall."

"We have to find that waste outlet Mrs Durcan's husband built. She told me you can walk through it, underneath the main wall to the outside."

Tubs winced. "Sounds yucky to me."

"Dobermanns or the yuck, Tubs?" said Caveman.

"Yuck."

In silent single file they retraced their steps past the Biological Preparation building, following the waste duct downhill until it eventually entered another taller, wider pipeline.

Yes! This has got to be the main pipe laid by Mr Durcan. Crossing his fingers he said confidently, "It only carries that waste veggie stuff from the vats."

"Are you sure there's no poo?" said Scruffy.

Zara shivered. "I can't believe this filth is chucked into the river."

"Did you expect Dunraven to flush it down his toilet?" said Caveman.

Ignoring the remark, she addressed Shane. "Can't we do something about this horrible pollution?"

"I've something in mind for that. Later."

Snoog let out a gentle whine.

"We forgot to feed him before we left," said Tubs, picking up the dog.

"He's your responsibility," said Zara.

"Like you, Zara," said Caveman, "he has to eat."

"I brought some biscuits for him," said Shane, relieved that whatever flowed in the pipeline was only a few millimetres deep and smelt of nothing more obnoxious than over-boiled veg.

After their short torch-lit walk, Shane was first to exit the pipe and clamber over a line of seaweed-coated rocks. He stood upright to see he was standing on the stretch of foreshore estuary where the Carrowbeg entered the Atlantic. Four hundred metres away, the familiar silhouette of *The Helm Cafe* showed against the skyline.

As Snoog urinated copiously, Shane clapped Scruffy on the back. "First in, last out."

Wiping his Nikes with handfuls of grass, Scruffy said, "It's my considered opinion that we could all be arrested for breaking and entering."

"No damage to person or property," replied Shane silkily.

"And full marks for finding this new way in," said Caveman. "We won't have to worry about those Dobermanns again."

"Again?" cried Tubs. He scanned their faces to see if they were serious. Realising they were, his arms dropped to his sides. "Are you two loony?"

"I reckon Dunraven is experimenting," said Scruffy, "boiling down the fly-traps to get some valuable substance or other."

"Like what?" demanded Shane.

"Some new antibiotic…" began Scruffy.

"… Or a chemical that could cure cancer." interjected Tubs.

Caveman nodded slowly. "They could be right, Shane."

"Let's get the lowdown on the flytraps first," said Shane. Tapping his backpack he added, "I've collected some pods."

"Maybe those seeds are worth a packet?" said Scruffy. "And Dunraven's exporting them?"

"To Mars?" said Zara.

"Got a better suggestion, Miss Hoity Toity?" said Caveman.

"Knock it off, you two. I know someone who might know about flytraps." Shane placed an arm around Tubs. "In the meanwhile, Professor McAuley, your next job is to gen up on GM plants and that kierogenic stuff..."

"... Cryogenic."

"... Then we link up in *The Helm,* as usual."

"I'm getting cold," said Scruffy, blowing on his hands.

"Ask Mrs Durcan for fluffier blankets," said Caveman, making no attempt to hide the sarcasm.

On the walk back to the chalets, Zara pulled Shane aside. "Something tells me Dunraven isn't looking for cancer cures. What do you reckon?"

"We might be on the right track but..."

"But what?"

"It's just a feeling..."

Chapter 11

As the doors of Westport House's Interpretative Centre closed, Professor Hughes prepared to address the combined pupils of St Columbanus and Sandymount High. He ran an exasperated hand across his brow, pretending he simply wasn't seeing a straggler scuttling in via the side exit; especially as he'd insisted that all students be seated early.

Shane's "Sorry-I'm-late-sir," call sounded more like a greeting than an apology as he ignored Mr Stubbs' scowl. Squeezing himself in between Tubs and Zara, he mumbled, "I was washing the dirt off those pods."

The Professor lifted a folder from the table. "Good morning all. I was impressed by the overall standard of your reports, but one pupil stands out above everybody else."

Many St Columbanus pupils rolled their eyes resignedly. Shane even gave Tubs a congratulatory nudge; his friend's top-of-the-class achievements were as predictable as sunrise. It wasn't a question of who came first, it was who came second. Tubs' marks rarely sank below 90%, except in art.

Professor Hughes announced, "First place goes to – Shane Donnegan."

Immediately on his feet, Mr Stubbs' sweeping glare aborted any eruption of disbelief. Standing behind and out of sight of Professor Hughes, his thunderous scowl left no one in any doubt that a triple detention awaited anyone who voiced dissent. As the moment peaked, then passed, he called, "Excuse me, Professor, but Finbar McAuley always takes first place and…."

"… No mistake; Master Donnegan's report is a revelation. Let the young man step forward."

As Shane self-consciously made his way up the aisle, he couldn't help but feel sorry for Tubs, who, despite his crestfallen appearance, was clapping enthusiastically. He also heard Brockenhurst call out, "My, oh, my; Donkey Dung's report is a *revelation*." Pause. "A *cheating revelation*."

Unaware that Shane would have been more than happy to scrape a bare pass in most subjects; especially history, the Professor continued. "Shane's historical span is remarkable as are his ideas on how knowledge was preserved by Ireland's ancient people. He suggests the country's early colonists, the Fomorians, built the original foundations of Westport House at least a thousand years before St Patrick's arrival. Because they left no written records, Shane proposes two theories on how ancient information was passed from generation to generation."

Professor Hughes paused, still oblivious to the sea of sceptical faces focused on Shane. "This young man suggests that the Fomorians used materials that were available in 1500 BC – string made from wool and leather. Tying knots of varying shapes into different positions, they stored information which was later reread by trained readers. However, wool and leather disintegrate."

He nodded at Shane before continuing. "Shane further proposes that astronomical data were chiselled into Fomorian Knowledge Stones that once were commonplace around Westport but this information was obliterated by our harsh winters." His voice tightened. "Shane, where did these remarkable ideas come from?"

Shane mumbled, "They, er, came to me as I was, er, walking around the Estate, sir..." His voice trailed away to an awkward silence.

The Professor's eyebrows rose. "Perhaps your father is an archaeologist? Or were you rummaging surreptitiously through the latest *Archaeological Review*, eh?"

It sounds like the Professor has swallowed a bigger dictionary than Tubs... he's obviously a nice guy but he's not to know Dad's a fisherman in Oz or...

Mistaking Shane's look of mystification for embarrassment, Professor Hughes addressed Mr Stubbs. "I don't recollect seeing this talented young man in your Scholarship Class? Anyway, Shane, please accept your prize, a copy of my latest publication, *Westport's Mysterious Past*." As he handed over the book, the Professor whispered, "Your ideas, Shane, are worthy of further discussion. Would a brief meeting tomorrow morning at ten suit? My business card etcetera are inside the book's cover."

Unsure of how to respond, Shane muttered, "Er, thanks for the prize, sir, and yeah, tomorrow's, er, fine; we've a free morning."

Returning to slump into his seat, he hoped Zara wouldn't notice that she could've fried eggs on his cheeks. He glanced down at the Westport House Visitor's Pass and the Professor's card which read:

Henry Sylvester Hughes
Professor of Archaeology; Astronomy; History.
Tel 087 1611580

Why would a professor, of all people, want to link up with me? About history of all things!

Chapter 12

The following morning, Shane and Tubs parked their bikes and dashed up the steps of Westport House. Inside the main doors, a cheerful young woman was waiting outside the wood-panelled library to confront them.

"You guys must have missed all those CLOSED TO THE PUBLIC signs?" she said, her voice mocking but friendly.

"We have an *official* appointment with Professor Hughes," announced Shane loftily, brandishing his pass.

"I'm Dr Connolly," she said, "curator of Westport House and *you,* Shane, have an appointment. Your friend doesn't; he stays down here. Professor Hughes is waiting in the Observatory upstairs."

"Thanks, Miss," he said, muttering under his breath.

He sauntered along the hallway lined with suits of armour, blunderbusses and swords, then passed beneath the tattered regimental flags that hung from the overhead marble gallery. Mounting the sweeping stairway, he filed past lines of landscape paintings, portraits of uniformed men and busts of people he assumed were famous and obviously long dead. By the time he'd reached the top floor, he'd seen enough grim depictions of battle scenes and cavalry charges to last him a lifetime.

Didn't they do anything else in history but fight and kill each other?

As he and Professor Hughes shook hands, Shane noted some of the pages on the Professor's desk were covered with mathematical calculations and geometrical shapes; others with alphabets and scripts that looked equally baffling.

"Thank you for coming, Shane," the Professor

said. "I have long researched the Fomorians; I suspect that you may also have some special interest?"

"To tell the truth, Professor, I'd never heard of them before our field trip."

"Yet your report strongly suggests that you possess a particular understanding of *those* ancient people…" The Professor pointed to the map on the wall.

Shane gave the map a cursory glance. "A lot of

Ancient Historic Locations Associated
with
The Fomorians

that Fomorian stuff," he said, "I got from my guide."

The Professor rubbed an itchy spot on his forehead. "Mm... this is rather puzzling, because we have no record of who that guide was." He ran his finger down a list of names. "The instructors that day were myself, Mr Stubbs, Dr Connolly and Patrick Slevin."

So how come neither Tubs nor the Professor saw my guide?

Unsure of what else to say, Shane pointed to the adjoining alcove where a long brass telescope sat, pointing to the sky. "I see you're interested in astrology, Professor," he said brightly, determined to make a good impression.

The Professor stiffened. "My field is Astronomy, the scientific study of the universe!" he snapped. "*Astrology* has the scientific content of a celebrity magazine; crackpot mumbo-jumbo for idiots!"

Oops, I thought astronomy and astrology were the same thing!

The Professor continued. "As Archaeological Director of Co Mayo, my team and I are currently excavating beneath Westport House where we've unearthed extensive tunnels, all of Fomorian origin. I'm also considered an expert in matters of the occult."

Shane's tongue flicked across his lips. "Do you mean, er, ghosts and stuff, sir?"

"Occult simply means mysterious phenomena that lack scientific explanation. Westport House was built on Grace O'Malley's sixteenth-century estate – on a site I've identified as Fomorian. This whole coastline was once a battleground between the strange forces of Ireland's earliest settlers, the Fomorians and their enemies, the Tuatha de Dannan."

"Er, what do you mean by *strange,* sir?"

The Professor placed his hands in a position of prayer against his lips and appeared unsure of whether to respond to Shane's question or avoid answering it. After a brief hesitation he resumed on a more enthusiastic note. "The few historical references to these people − written over a thousand years after the Fomorians' disappearance − are highly unreliable, describing our early ancestors as *arriving from the sky* and being *well versed in magic.* Also, many of the rock inscriptions around Westport House, Croagh Patrick and the surrounding countryside appear to depict stars, so..."

"... Are you saying the Fomorians came from outer space, Professor?" said Shane, fighting a smile. "Sounds a bit Star Trek-ish."

The Professor chuckled. "No, Shane, I'm merely emphasising that despite their keeping astronomical records, we know virtually nothing about them."

This is a good time to ask...

"I wonder could you help me identify something, sir?"

"Of course."

Shane removed a flytrap pod from his rucksack. "During our, er, field trip, we picked up this strange thing near Lord Dunraven's industrial buildings. I was sort of wondering what it is."

The Professor scrutinised the long green husk. "Umm, looks very odd. I will sound out the University's Botany Department..." The bleeping from the red light on the desk cut in and the Professor rose quickly. "I'm sorry to terminate our meeting so soon, Shane – an emergency fire drill − would you care to join my excavation this Sunday morning? We could continue our discussion then?"

"Well, er, yes, Professor, thanks."

"Here's your permit and high vis jacket. Thank you for coming."

Tubs was patrolling the main hallway as Shane descended the stairway to the main entrance. "Well?" he demanded.

"Professor Hughes is seriously hung up on the Fomorians."

"Those ancient cannibals you were rabbitin' on about in your report?"

"Can you believe he's invited me to go *ex-cav-at-ing* with him? Fancy coming along Sunday?"

Shane heard the relief in Tubs' voice. "Count me out; we're all off to the movies; much more excitin' than starin' at rocks."

Chapter 13

From *The Helm Cafe's* window seat, Shane watched Tubs approach, a sheaf of papers under his arm, his pink cheeks brighter than usual.

"It's big stuff," Tubs jabbered excitedly as he entered.

"Explain in lingo we can all follow," said Scruffy.

"No fancy jawbreakers," said Zara.

Wiping wispy blond hair from his forehead, Tubs deliberately fell silent. When satisfied he was the centre of everyone's attention, he hooked his thumbs behind his lapels. "Ladies and gentlemen of the jury," he began in an exaggerated, haughty voice, "GM stands for genetic modification, like when scientists take genes from fish livin' around the North Pole and transplant them into strawberries." He looked around the table, awaiting a response.

"But why?" said Zara eventually.

"Bad weather kills strawberries but the fish genes enable the strawberries to keep growin', even in winter."

Scruffy nodded. "More spondoolix for the strawberry farmers."

Caveman bullishly folded his arms. "If that's the future, you can stuff it."

Tubs continued unabashed. "I reckon Dunraven has genetically modified those flytrap things into giant plants and they need to guzzle meat to keep growin'."

A shout came from behind. Brockenhurst stood in the doorway. "Shane," he called gruffly. "I propose a truce."

He looks as if he's slept in a ditch. That's the first half-friendly word I've ever heard from Brockenhurst.

Shane strode towards the door, feigning a

nonchalance he didn't remotely feel. "What's up, er, Jeremy?" he asked, balancing his weight on his toes, his guard slightly raised.

"I've come to warn you – don't set foot in Dunraven's gaff. It's seriously dangerous."

Taken aback by Brockenhurst's absence of hostility, Shane felt a twinge of sympathy. *Keep schtum about last night...* "Why?" he asked.

The corners of Brockenhurst's mouth twitched. "Myself and the lads popped into Dunraven's last night. A giant plant ate my dog!"

Shane feigned amazement. "You're joking – didn't you report it?"

"I've just been to the Garda Station..." As his tongue flicked across his lips, Brockenhurst's face had taken on the haunted look of someone who had never quite seen eye to eye with the forces of law and order. "The sergeant told me to hop it, otherwise they'd do me for trespassing. Keep away from Dunraven's place."

"Well, er, thanks, Jeremy..." began Shane but Brockenhurst had already walked off without a backward glance.

After hearing Brockenhurst's account, Caveman said, "The cops are obviously in Dunraven's paws."

"Or they reckon his place is legit," said Zara.

"It's not illegal to experiment with plants," said Scruffy.

"Forget Brockenhurst," said Shane, "it's time Tubs told us about cryogenics."

Tubs made a further fuss of fiddling with his paperwork before continuing. "Cryogenics means keepin' things at temperatures way below freezin' so it's used in hospitals to keep body parts fresh for transplant operations. In California, for a truckful of dollars, you can have your body preserved in this cryogenic stuff for hundreds of years."

"Why?" demanded Scruffy.

"If they find some way of prolongin' life in the future then – bingo – you can be resurrected!"

Caveman cracked his knuckles.

"The usual cryogenic stuff is liquid nitrogen," continued Tubs, "it's stored at minus two hundred and…"

Shane cut in by clapping Tubs on the back. "Great stuff, Tubs. But what does Dunraven want with GM plants and cryogenics?"

Nobody answered.

"Only one way to find out then," said Shane, in best businesslike tone.

"How?" mumbled Tubs.

"By going back to Dunraven's," said Caveman with obvious relish.

"Are you two crazy?" demanded Scruffy.

"I'd rather die," said Tubs.

Shane nudged Scruffy. "Just one visit. You can bring your piggybank, Scruff, count your dosh while we're looking around, OK?"

Scruffy couldn't conceal his grin. "Oh, that's good, Shane. OK, OK. It's my opinion that we pay one more visit. *One.*"

"You never did listen to common sense, Shane," said Tubs, arms dropping to his sides. "*One* very short visit; the day after tomorrow."

Zara's full-headlight glare focused on Shane. "I just hope you know what you're doing, Shane Donnegan."

So do I…

Chapter 14

Torch in hand and wearing a safety helmet, Shane stood behind Professor Hughes. For fifteen minutes they'd made their way below the foundations of Westport House and had come to a halt in a low-ceilinged tunnel, lined on both sides by dilapidated nineteenth-century dungeons. Its uneven floor comprised rounded stones and irregular cobbles while rusty chains and manacles lined some of the damp walls. Many of the collapsed cells were boarded-up with KEEP OUT – DANGER signs. Ahead, the passageway was blocked by a wall of rubble.

"Follow me," said the Professor, squeezing past the obstruction and descending a further series of steps into another low-ceilinged underpass. "This is my new investigation site," he continued, his flashlight illuminating the low roof and the nearby pathway. "You are now standing close to what I believe was a Fomorian religious site, Shane, partially destroyed by a minor earthquake. Perhaps by undersea volcanic activity."

"Where do those passageways go, Professor?" he said with faint interest.

"I haven't yet investigated. One definitely leads to the coast, the other may connect with Clare Island, even the Aran Islands. These corridors were once frequented by many people."

"What are those things for?" Shane said, pointing to the sheets of rectangular glass that lined each side of the passage.

The Professor's serious eyes locked with Shane's. "This is strictly between you and me, Shane. Understood?"

"Er, yes, of course, Professor."

"What you are seeing are identification systems I

designed when working with the American Central Intelligence Agency. I call them *auro-magneto-scopes,* AMSs. Based on the most advanced metal detectors and x-ray scanners, they measure the body heat and genetic profile of every living creature that passes. Aside from identifying fox, rat and mink, they recently recorded humans who are of European origin yet possess Bronze Age DNA."

His interest increasing as he tried to get his head around the full significance of the Professor's words, Shane licked his lips.

"The AMSs," the Professor continued, "also logged a particularly tall, muscular male but the thunderstorm outside somehow corrupted the readings. I later found bloodstains on the cobbles but despite their being contaminated by rat droppings, I was able to provisionally establish that this man had only one eye and his DNA was 100% Ancient Greek. Do you have views on this, Shane?"

"*Me?*"

"Yes, Shane, you."

Unsure of how to respond, Shane hesitated. "Er, did the batteries of your auro-thingies go flat? Maybe rain seeped in from somewhere?"

The Professor shook his head. "Each AMS is waterproofed and is re-charged daily."

"Did the AMSs spot anything else?"

"Recently two humans, each with virtually identical, modern Germanic DNA, were recorded. I know Lord Dunraven employs EU workers on his Industrial Complex but nobody from above can gain access here..."

"… Dunraven's workers are hardly connected with your Fomorians, sir?"

The Professor broke the lengthening silence. "A

snippet from the latest *Archaeological Review* might be relevant."

"How?" said Shane, his curiosity increasing despite himself.

"During the war in Iraq, American planes bombed a desert cave containing hidden rolls of parchment written in Ancient Greek. After many years, the fragments have finally been pieced together and they shed light on the Fomorians."

"In *Iraq*? Thousands of miles away?"

"The scrolls describe a cave-dwelling race in Ireland called the *Fo Morians*. Translated from Ancient Irish, *Fo* means under and *Moire* means the sea – underwater dwellers. Supposedly powerful swimmers, these people were also formidable fighters who could speak different languages at birth and traded with Ancient Greece."

"So your Fomorians didn't come from the stars after all?" said Shane, smiling, but his attempt to lighten up things went unnoticed by the Professor, who was extracting an iPad from his holdall.

"Excuse me, Shane, while I log last night's recorded data from the AMSs."

Rather than be bored to death by hanging around the grim surroundings, Shane ambled along the passageway, his torch picking out the narrow alleyways and cul-de-sacs that dotted the labyrinth. Sixty metres further on, he realised he was approaching a dead end and glanced over his shoulder; the Professor was still engrossed, his torchlight slicing into the intervening blackness like a golden knife blade.

The barrier blocking Shane's way was one of vertical rock but as he drew closer, he saw it comprised two tall upright slabs separated by a long, well concealed, central cleft. Taking a deep breath, he squeezed and wriggled his way with difficulty through the cramped fissure to find himself standing inside a dusty circular vault. Constructed entirely from limestone, tall, roughly-hewn boulders lined the sides of the claustrophobic crypt which dovetailed into a domed canopy of long slates, four metres above his head. From the centre of the roof, a large stone eye stared sightlessly downward.

This place stinks of stale air and history...

He stared open-mouthed at the strange carvings on the surrounding rocks. Without warning, his torch slipped and hit the floor with a noise that sounded explosively loud. The darkness was total and except for his thudding heart; so was the thunderous silence. In the centre of the chamber stood a roughly-shaped plinth, bordered by two large basins, all carved from stone. His eyes were drawn to the dusty wooden box lying on the plinth, as if it were the only thing of importance in the vault. His hold on reality began to slip as the thought struck him like a sledgehammer – *How come I can see these things in the dark?*

Picking up the torch, he took two forward steps and jammed the box under his arm. Scraping knees and knuckles as he backtracked through the aperture, he imagined voices were spewing ancient curses at him for his sacrilegious intrusion. The Professor was smiling and rubbing his palms together as Shane returned. "I have now positively identified three different types of human DNA – Bronze Age, Ancient Greek and modern Germanic. Speaking of DNA..." He handed Shane a small bag. "That bizarre pod you gave me shares many similarities with the *Dionaea muscipula*..."

"... What's that, Professor?"

"The Venus flytrap – but your pod's DNA is

totally unique."

"What do you mean?"

"It has never been previously recorded – anywhere! The size of the mature plant must be mindboggling. I've forwarded copies of its DNA to Harvard and Cambridge for further analyses. Are you quite sure you found this on the Estate?"

"Defo, sir, Dunraven has a field full of those, er, plants." *Don't mention the dog...* Incapable of suppressing his excitement any longer, he blurted, "Look at what I just found, Professor." He laid the wooden box on the nearby boulder, under the full glare of his torch.

The Professor stared reverently at the container for some seconds then moved forward to scrape away the accumulated grime of centuries from the lid. "Where did you get... this?" he whispered.

"On an altar in a..."

"... It's *empty!*" Unable to conceal his disappointment, the Professor added, "It must have housed something important – otherwise why leave it on an... an altar, you say?"

"Look, Professor, there's things written on the lid and along the side," cried Shane but his voice trailed off. "Sorry, Professor, it's not writing, it's just, em, signs and squiggles – burnt into the wood – and huge eyes..."

The Professor refocused his torchlight on the box. "These baffling hieroglyphs do not ring *any* linguistic bells for me. The box is made from ebony; a rare and expensive wood; not available in ancient Ireland, it was imported from Africa, most likely Egypt." His voice dropped. "This container must once have housed something of great importance. Show me where you found it, Shane, then we head back and send it off for immediate analysis."

Chapter 15

Shane sullenly watched rivulets of water run down *The Helm's* windows, while peals of thunder grumbled dully in the distance. The weather had put his plans on hold and Mr Stubbs had cancelled all site visits, suggesting the students used the free time to continue with writing up their essays. Worse still, Shane knew the downpours might mean a rise in the level of the Carrowbeg, threatening to obliterate their new entrance to the Estate.

Dishcloth burst from the kitchen, carrying a toolbox and an umbrella. "I've just had a call from Dunraven," he said breathlessly. "Lightning's banjaxed his main compressor, so I'm rigging him up a spare and taking over the lunchtime grub. I'll be away for four hours, minimum. How about you wasters running the cafe while I'm away?"

"How much an hour?" piped up Scruffy.

"What! You guys owe me a lorry load of favours; free pizza and chips, free coke..."

"... How much an hour?" insisted Scruffy.

"Er, well, five euros."

"Seven-fifty and it's a deal," said Scruffy silkily.

"That's daylight robbery..."

"... Any chance," interrupted Shane, "of me and Tubs going with you, Dishcloth? Just to take a quick squizz around Dunraven's place?" *Best not mention anything about our previous visit...*

"This is work, Shane, not teenage fooling around."

"If you take Tubs and me with you," said Shane, "the gang will happily run the cafe. Eight euros an hour; plus meals and tips."

"Blackmail!" Dishcloth spluttered. "What will

you lot be like as adults? Probably end up running the Mafia. OK, it's a deal. Bring your rain gear."

Crouched behind boxes of packed lunches and soft drinks, Shane watched the countryside slide past as the van headed for the rear entrance to the Estate. As they passed the large, open-armed statue of St Patrick, Dish-cloth pointed. "It's a pity that holy man is not alive today to teach you robbers some decent values..."

Rain was ringing off the tiles of the entrance hut as the Transit pulled up under the sign:

DUNRAVEN BIOLOGICAL PRODUCTS
CONTACT LENS SOLUTIONS

As the oil-skinned gatekeeper emerged from the security hut, Dishcloth wound down the window. "Dirty morning, Jimbo."

"Mr Cartwright is expecting you, Vinny; the Phase 2 Building."

"What's Phase 2?"

"Haven't a clue. I is on gate security and that's what I knows about, gate security."

Inside the walls of Dunraven's industrial complex, all Shane could identify through the windscreen wipers were islands of isolated woodland connected by straight concrete avenues with no obvious exterior lighting. With the exception of the tall, glass-fronted HQ, all buildings were long and windowless, surrounded by copses of young pines, unlike the ancient woodlands that dominated most of the Estate. In the distance, he could vaguely make out the upper stories of Westport House.

"This area was once a holiday camp," said Dish-cloth gloomily, "packed with kids and caravans. Looks like an army base now."

Shane drew a quick intake of breath. Standing beside the sign, PHASE 2, two guards stood. Despite being similarly dressed in oilskins and boots, the men's appearance and build were almost mirror images of each other.

Dishcloth lowered the van window. "'Morning, guys, Lord Dunraven's expecting me."

Unsmiling, one of the guards marched forward, glanced through the half-opened window then waved the van forward. As he accelerated past, Dishcloth muttered under his breath, "And a *very* good morning to you, too, misery-guts. Bit of manners never harmed anyone."

Dishcloth parked in front of a low, featureless metallic building that again reminded Shane of an aircraft hangar. "Keep down," he grated as he opened the rear doors and manoeuvred the cumbersome compressor to the ground. "Thanks for the great help, lads," he called sarcastically to the guards.

The nearest guard sprung forward. "Achtung," he shouted angrily.

"What's your problem?" said Dishcloth, frowning.

Shane held his breath as the guard onehandedly wrenched the compressor from Dishcloth's grip and pointed to an entrance some distance further along the building.

"Use zat door," he growled.

Dishcloth wordlessly walked back to the van and returned quickly, carrying sandwiches and two cans of 7Up which he handed to the guards. "Those might cheer you lads up," he said.

Shane could see how chuffed the guards were as they tore off the cellophane wrappers and voraciously slurped down the drinks like parched children after a long walk. Still chewing contentedly, one of the guards pointed Dishcloth to the front entrance and made a slicing action across his neck.

"Achtung," he said, sounding almost friendly. He picked up a large pebble, held it above the entrance mat then let it slip from his fingers. As the stone struck, the doormat shot aside, a yawning rectangular pit appeared and the sound of rock striking metal echoed from below.

As Dishcloth gazed open-mouthed into the deep trough, the guard waved an admonishing finger. "Danger, kamerad," he said softly.

Shane watched as Dishcloth, aided by both guards, together pushed the compressor into the main building. "Tubs, doesn't *achtung* mean...?"

"... It's German for *look out*."

"Why do the guards all look the same? And why are they speaking German?"

"From the same German family maybe? Nah; that doesn't add up."

"Those guards will be looking over Dishcloth's shoulder for the next few hours; let's do a quick recce. The place is deserted."

"I'll wait in the van."

"Come on, Tubs, there's no risk."

Keeping to the trees whenever possible, their half-hour exploration of the grounds was uneventful because all buildings were locked and they felt far too exposed to venture far. On returning to the vehicle, Tubs stopped outside the Phase 2 building and stepping backwards, attempted to remove something from inside his raincoat.

Shane had spotted the danger but it was too late. Too intent on opening the bar of chocolate, Tubs had allowed his heel to come into contact with the second concealed trap. The innocuous doormat shot to the side and Tubs toppled, totally off balance. In a blur, Shane was aside the opening, his right arm shot out, caught the back of Tub's mackintosh and wrenched him upwards. With his left hand, he simultaneously grasped the rear end of Tubs' jeans and in the same sweep, slammed him into a standing position, away from the lip of the trap.

His mouth dangling open, Tubs was unsure of what had happened; the whole incident was over so quickly that he had no time to feel anxiety or fear. Only gratitude.

"Achtung, kamerad," said Shane smilingly in a mock-German accent. "It is safer in ze van."

"Tha... thanks, Shane," was all Tubs could say before asking in a hushed voice, "How did you... how could you... move so... so quickly?"

"Wish I knew, Tubs."

Chapter 16

A further half hour passed before Dishcloth returned and flopped back into the driving seat. "Those guards wouldn't let me go for a pee and that manager Cartwright is an unmannerly pig. What about those hidden traps, eh?"

As they motored towards the exit, Tubs checked they were out of Dishcloth's earshot then nudged Shane. "No way am I comin' back here. We could be wanderin' around in the dark and..." He shuddered and didn't elaborate.

Shane winced, imagining fractured bone protruding through the severed muscles of his friend's leg. *Unless I've Tubs on board, then Zara and Scruffy will cop out.*

"If we had a map of the place, Tubs, would you come back with me?"

Tubs' eyes narrowed. "What sort of map?"

"A plan or a drawing of Dunraven's factory complex − something showing where everything is? Would you be happy?"

"Well, I, er, suppose so..."

"...That's settled then."

"Where would you get a map like that?"

"Leave that to me."

On the return journey to *The Helm*, Shane asked Dishcloth to drop them off on Westport's Doris Bridge. "It's not far," he whispered to Tubs, setting off at a brisk pace.

"Keepin' things to yourself as usual?" said Tubs, trying to keep up.

"No, I'm thinking about what I'm going to say..." *Mrs Durcan told me that all local building info is kept in the County Chambers. The last time we were lucky getting around Dunraven's in the dark; the next time will need far more planning... Ah, there he goes!*

Outside the County Chambers, Shane saw the heron float like a grey ghost over the Carrowbeg. He knew the bird always alighted in the same place before stepping into the current where it remained thigh deep and motionless, until some hapless aquatic creature swam past. Faster than the blink of an eye, the bird would strike and with something wriggling in its beak, depart as silently as it had come. *My karate teacher was right, I must be patient. Like that heron...*

After passing through the County Chambers' revolving doors, he looked around the spacious hall, unsure of where to go.

"Can I help you lads?" said the porter kindly, laying down his newspaper.

"We're looking for the *Building & Engineering* section, sir," said Shane, flashing his 200-watt smile.

The porter directed him to the counter with the nameplate: *Ms E Ramsbottom, Planning Manageress.* "I'd go carefully if I were you, lads," he said. "She's having one of her days."

Shane played a rapid tattoo on the buzzer with his finger. Ms Ramsbottom appeared almost instantaneously and she wasn't buying Shane's friendly beam.

"This is NOT a fire station," she fumed.

Shane waited a few seconds for tempers to cool then courteously explained to the simmering official that all he required was an up-to-date drawing of the buildings inside the Westport Estate.

"It's part of our school holiday project," he explained silkily. *Not exactly a million miles from the truth.*

Over the rims of her half-moon glasses, she

levelled a gaze at him that would have cracked concrete. "Such information," she snapped, "is not available to minors. Good day." Rolling her eyes, she flounced back into the office.

"I'd run along now lads, if I were you," whispered the porter. "That short fuse of hers does be getting shorter in the bad weather."

"Thanks, sir," said Shane, trying to hide his disappointment. Under his breath he whispered to Tubs "I bet she trained as a prison guard."

Making no attempt to disguise his glee, Tubs said, "No map means no goin' back to Dunraven's, right?"

Shane wasn't listening, he was staring at the heron's vacant fishing spot. "Tomorrow afternoon we all head off to Murrisk to climb Croagh Patrick," he said. He suddenly rubbed his hands together. "I've another plan."

Tubs frowned. "What?"

Shane grinned. "I'll explain at the top of the mountain."

***

In blazing afternoon sunshine, both the St Columbanus and Sandymount High groups had completed the long climb to the top of Croagh Patrick and were enjoying the welcome rest. Under Mr Stubbs' watchful eye, most were wolfing down sandwiches, taking selfies or horsing around near the whitewashed chapel that dominated the mountain top. Caveman and Scruffy were in the middle of a serious stone-throwing completion. Most of the other pupils lazed around or were gazing at the sparkling panorama of mountain, sky and sea that stretched into the hazy distance.

Standing close to the lip of the summit, Shane was

engrossed in surveying the countryside – some 750m below – through binoculars.

"What are you gawkin' at?" asked Tubs, munching happily.

Shane didn't respond but handed over the field glasses to Zara. "This is where you come in," he said. "You can see the whole of Westport Estate from up here so…" He extracted a sketch pad and a set of coloured pencils from his backpack. "You're tops in art so how about drawing us a nifty map of the Estate to include Dunraven's complex?"

"Why not take photos, dumbo?" said Tubs.

"Too far away to get a proper shot. Dishcloth says Dunraven sleeps in Westport House but spends the rest of his time in his HQ. We need Zara to give us a rough layout of where everything is."

For thirty seconds Zara studied the distant terrain with the binoculars. "It shouldn't take me long," she breezed.

"Be sure to mark those entry traps," said Tubs.

Half an hour later, Shane whistled appreciatively as she handed over her neat, multi-coloured sketch of the Estate which included everything of importance from Dunraven's HQ complex to the perimeter walls of Westport House itself.

Even Tubs, despite being rubbish at art, was impressed.

"I wasn't *exactly* sure where those burglar pits were," she said apologetically.

Shane punched the air. "We'll be on the lookout for them, Zara. This map is brill; we're set up for our evening visit."

Zara's Map

Chapter 17

The recent downpours had made the entry to the Estate so slippery that Shane had to almost force Snoog into Mr Durcan's dank tunnel.

This time Dunraven's somehow feels spookier. Last visit I didn't know what to expect, this time I do, or at least I think I do...

Following the landmarks on Zara's map, they exited the wastepipe in single file and keeping to the woods, skirted the Fly Trap field, bypassed the Phase I structure and arrived at a second large building signposted:

PHASE 2
CLONING STATION
AUTHORISED PERSONNEL ONLY

"This is the place we visited with Dishcloth," muttered Tubs, stepping apprehensively around the entrance mats. He switched on his decoder while the others hung back in the shadows.

"What *exactly* is cloning, Tubs?" said Scruffy.

"After takin' a single cell from somethin' livin', scientists reproduce exact copies of it in the lab. They've already done it with sheep, cows, dogs..."

Caveman cut in. "... Sounds Frankenstein-ish to me."

Tubs straightened his glasses. "If you just *opened* a book ..." he began. Seeing Caveman's smouldering eyes he added quickly, "Sorry, Mike I was only foolin'."

Shane led the way along the side of the long metal structure which appeared identical to the windowless Biological Building. Tubs decoded the lock to reveal an anteroom lined with lab coats, protective suits and white wellingtons. A glass door opened to the left; stairs led upwards.

"Dishcloth says this whole building is soundproofed," whispered Shane, bounding up the stairs then waving the others to follow.

Caveman warily scanned the empty storeroom. "Why's the whole floor made of glass?"

"Ask Dunraven," said Zara sweetly.

"No squabbling, guys," murmured Shane.

Under his feet lay a spacious laboratory, its illuminated walls lined by computers, the floor with metallic, sterile-looking equipment. White-coated personnel patrolled, many carrying clipboards or iPads. He was aware of how the lab's lights from below intensified his friends' drawn faces. *This place reminds me of a futuristic scene from some Sci-Fi film...*

"Watch out," said Zara, pulling Shane towards the shadows. "Anyone looking up will see..."

"Relax," Shane said, getting used to the unnerving sensation of being able to walk unnoticed over other people's heads. "Dishcloth filled me in about Dunraven's spying gizmos – we can see down, they can't see up."

Caveman pointed. "Look, they're filling those test tubes on the trolley with that flytrap juice."

"We do have eyes, thank you," said Zara.

All gazed as a guard pushed the laden trolley into the adjoining bay, where a row of goggled workers in protective gear sat on a long bench, all using pipettes to insert something into each test tube.

Tubs moistened his lips. "They're shovin' trays of tubes into that black octopus thing ..." His voice trailed off.

Five metal steps led to the central metallic apparatus that dominated the laboratory. Fed from the front and rear by an array of cables and wires, its bulbous exterior was dotted with dials and timers. A short distance away, another team sat staring at a bank of computer screens.

As the light above the apparatus began to pulsate bright green, a technician opened the circular door and stepped inside. Quickly reappearing through a cloud of swirling steam, he was pushing a trolley laden with test tubes. Two figures in protective suits slotted each tube into individual containers, each the shape and size of a cigar cylinder, all of which were immediately boxed, labelled and taken outside.

Tubs nudged Shane. "I saw somethin' like this when they cloned Dolly."

"Who's Dolly?"

"The first ever cloned sheep. It was on the Discovery Channel…"

"… The lights have just come on over there," interrupted Scruffy.

Shane's attention was taken by two men in business suits who'd entered the room adjacent to the lab, marked *Directors' Office*. One stood while the other switched on a computer and slouched behind his desk, chewing on a large cigar.

"We can't hear a thing," whispered Shane, trying to conceal his exasperation.

Tubs extracted what appeared to be a compact dictation recorder from his backpack. "I was expectin' such problems," he said theatrically, "so this is my own scattered-light laser monitor or narrowband FM receiver…"

"… Skip the fancy stuff, McAuley," growled Caveman. "What does it do?"

"Usin' a little Blue Tack, I stick my tiny parabolic

microphone to the glass – like so – connect it to my receiver and, SHAZZAM! – the tiny oscillations of the glass produced by the conversation below are translated into what's being said." He proudly handed the earphones to Shane.

The first voice sounded English and was well spoken:

"...the last batch was two percent, so stop worrying."

"He claimed he'd drown me if I don't get a five percent success rate with his genetically modified extract."

"Come on, Claude, he was only joking."

"Ever hear Dunraven crack a joke?"

"Look, I wasn't director on the Dolly Project for nothing. Granted his flytrap extract does produce quirky amino acids but cloning failures are not your fault."

Shane held his breath as the speaker leant back in his chair to relight his cigar.

"You never did take to Dunraven, eh?"

"I want to tell him to do the genetic splicing himself if he thinks..."

"... Nobody expects you to fall in love with him, Claude. Think of the money. Here, look at the figures yourself. Where did Dunraven get his cloning prototype?"

"He dug him out of a WW II military graveyard in Berlin. Panzer tank commander, Kurt von Somebody-or-other. Highly decorated; Iron Cross, Knight's Cross, etcetera. Mind you, Dunraven's von So-and-sos are strong as bulls, bilingual, work eighteen hours a day..."

"... It's a shame that excess heat, flu or Covid kills them after six months. You know he was a whizz-kid at NASA, Harry?"

"He's either a genius or a serious weirdo."

"Who cares, Claude? Oodles of dollars. He even supplied the kidney for Westport's Inspector McNamara's transplant."

The man behind the desk stood up and laid papers on the table. *"There's the figures for tomorrow's meeting. Let's go."*

Shane watched the men depart, leaving their papers on the desk and the room in darkness. His hands were trembling.

Seeing he was more in shock than in thought, Zara asked softly, "What were they saying, Shane? Shane!"

He heard the words but his mind was unable to process them. "I want to see those Directors' papers before I say anything. I'll only be a few minutes; I know where the side entrance is..."

The four friends waited, craning nervously, but were unable to see anything in the Directors' Room until Shane's torch came on, showing him hunched beneath the table. With the Directors' computer at his side, he was taking snapshots of papers spread across his knees.

"Why's he under the table?" grumbled Caveman.

"Why do you think?" said Zara witheringly.

It took twelve everlastingly long minutes before gaunt-faced Shane returned. "Dunraven is cloning humans," he said matter-of-factly, "then selling their organs for surgical spare parts."

All stood in silence, trying to grasp the enormity of what he'd said.

"Clonin'... *humans*...?" croaked Tubs.

"I've just photographed the Directors' papers and nicked their computer stick." He held up the USB.

"All those guards must be clones," mumbled Scruffy.

"Wait!" cried Zara. "If Dunraven's producing humans for spare parts, what happens to what's left behind?"

"It becomes wheelbarrow meat," said Caveman, cracking his knuckles.

I've dragged us into this horror. It's up to me to get us out of it.

Shane said in a low voice, "The leftovers are fed to the plants which are boiled down to help start the cloning business all over again."

"How much would Dunraven get for a heart?" said Scruffy.

"A quarter of a million dollars," said Shane. "Same for a kidney; this week he's shipping twenty to Tokyo via Shannon Airport."

"How would he get that stuff through customs?" said Caveman.

"In refrigerated cases of contact lens solution," said Zara impatiently.

"It's time to bring in the police," said Scruffy.

"Brockenhurst has already tried," said Shane. "Anyway, who would anyone believe – Lord Dunraven or us?"

Zara chewed her lip. "Let's photograph everything. Now."

After they'd taken numerous shots and videos, Shane checked the results. "Useless," he said, trying to hide his disappointment. "None of these clearly show what's really going on. We'll have to borrow Dishcloth's fancy camera to get good close-ups. Then we present convincing stuff to the Guards..."

"... And put the best video on TikTok," added Zara.

Shane called over Snoog and opened the buckle

of the dog's identification neckband. He jammed the USB into the plastic slot holding the dog's particulars, closed the clasp then replaced the collar. "Just in case anything happens to us, we all know where the evidence is." He punched the air. "Tomorrow night we burst open Dunraven's barrel of tricks."

Chapter 18

Late the following evening, the five friends were still hanging around Westport's deserted harbour, itching for darkness to fall before sneaking into the Estate.

"The river's gone a funny colour," Zara muttered.

Tubs didn't glance up from his phone. "It's the sunset glintin' off the water, your ladyship."

"I've two eyes in my head, Finbar McAuley; that water's turning R, E, D – red."

"Maybe you need contact lenses," Caveman butted in.

Zara wrinkled her nose. "It also smells."

Shane set down Dishcloth's camera case and stared into the current. Moments later he straightened, fists clenched. "Zara's right. It's Dunraven's stinking waste – wiping out the wildlife on this stretch of river." *This the heron's favourite fishing spot!*

"Can't *we* do something?" said Zara, tugging Shane's sleeve.

"Patience," said Shane grimly.

After finally entering the Estate, Shane halted on the bridge below the lake. Leaning over the parapet, he shone his torch downwards. "That's where Dunraven's filth goes into the river – if Caveman and me can shift that wastepipe into that smaller brook nearby, then everything will flow in the opposite direction – back into the gardens of Westport House."

"Isn't that sad," said Zara, smiling. "Dunraven's prize roses will get watered by his own filthy yuck."

As Shane signalled Caveman to join him, Scruffy stepped forward, his arm raised. "This carry-on is another criminal offence…" he began.

"Wiping out fish and birds is the criminal offence,

pal," Shane shot back. Jabbing Scruffy in the chest with his finger, he added, "In my book, protecting them is perfectly legit. Got that?"

Never having seen Shane ever lose his cool, the others averted their eyes then watched in silence as he and Caveman clambered down the rocky incline under torchlight. Close to the discharging wastepipe, the pair stripped down to their undies, and in bare feet waded into the water. After they'd scooped away sufficient shingle and long grass, Caveman slid his arms beneath the plastic pipe and attempted to shift it.

It didn't budge.

"Let me have a go," said Shane.

He inhaled deeply and bending low, cradled the pipe between his naked torso and arms. With a sudden upward wrench, he tore it free from its shallow trench and shunting it to the right, allowed the duct to sink into the adjacent stream.

After the grime-spattered pair had washed themselves clean in the river and dressed themselves, Caveman turned his puzzled gaze to Shane. "Where did you get the strength to lift that?" he said softly.

"Aunt Agnes' porridge," Shane said with a conspiratorial wink.

***

From the upstairs storeroom of the Cloning Lab, Shane studied the bustling activity in below. "There's something seriously big going down this weekend," he muttered.

Re-packing Dishcloth's camera, Tubs said, "We have enough photos to bring in the army."

Zara's steely voice butted in. "One of us should shoot off with the evidence."

110

"I'll go," volunteered Tubs instantly.

"And who'll decode the locks?" said Shane. "Zara's idea; she goes. Take Snoog, Zara, he's getting very jittery. Get Dishcloth to check that everything's OK with that USB then..."

"... Then off to the police," she said, picking up the dog.

"They mightn't believe you, Zara..." began Scruffy.

"... They will," she said, breathing loudly through her nose.

Checking that Zara was out of earshot, Tubs whispered, "She's got a serious mouth on her when she wants to."

"Tell me about it," grunted Caveman.

Standing outside in the shadow of the lab, Shane held Zara's gaze. "Be careful," he whispered. He heard the catch in her voice as she said goodbye and he remained staring wordlessly into the darkness after she'd been swallowed by the night.

"You OK?" whispered Caveman, clocking that Shane's earlier enthusiasm had been replaced by a palpable air of concern.

Shane folded Zara's map and pointed to the building in the distance. "Seven kinds of hell will break loose if anybody sees us now, Caveman."

In the lead, he jogged ahead through the silent woods without the aid of a torch until they reached the long metallic structure. Similar in size and construction to the other buildings they'd investigated, the plaque over the doorway read:

PHASE 3
GESTATION STATION
AUTHORISED PERSONNEL ONLY

"Everyone be on the lookout for carpet traps," warned Shane.

"What the hell's gestation?" grunted Caveman.

"It's the time a baby stays inside its mother," whispered Tubs, giving Caveman a friendly nudge.

Although he didn't know what to expect inside the building, Shane had a feeling it wasn't going to be pleasant. More secluded, set in denser woodland, it lay some distance back from the road. "This is our last stop, OK?" he said.

All nodded, including Caveman.

Tubs double-checked the ground around the entrance before decoding the lock. The main door slid open to reveal an anteroom, paved entirely in white tile. A wide wooden counter ran around the square-shaped foyer on which stood individual black and white photographs, each depicting random streaks and spirals.

Tubs pointed. "They're showin' collisions between subatomic particles," he explained, sucking air between his front teeth.

"Encyclopaedia time, Tubs?" said Caveman as he tried to push open the windowed door leading into the laboratory. It was locked and despite Tubs' efforts, remained so.

"What's the problem, Tubs?" said Shane.

"It's centrally locked."

"Damn."

Dejectedly Shane scanned the array of clocks, dials and meters that covered the walls on each side of the door. He read off the nearest row of gauges; *Heart Rate, Pulse, Oxygen Concentration, Potassium Level.* "What's going on in there?" he muttered, staring into the dark interior, shielding his eyes from the glaring electric light above.

He could make out rows of individual glass containers. Each the size of a microwave appliance, they reminded him of maternity-ward incubators he'd seen on TV. The fluid-filled vessels were fed by a series of wires and tubes while rotating beams of red light intermittently pulsated through the blue-green solutions. He hypnotically watched a large bubble, suspended as if by magic in the centre of the nearest container, ascend through the liquid. A cold hand clasped his heart as he followed its every movement until it reached the surface, then burst and disappeared.

There's something alive in every container! No, I must be imagining things…

"I'm going to stop whatever horror's going on in there," he said grimly, removing the walkie-talkie from his rucksack.

"Where did you get that?" demanded Tubs.

"I, er, borrowed it from the Biological Section."

"Nicked it, you mean," said Caveman. "What are you going to do with it?"

"I'll pretend to be Dunraven and stop his consignment from leaving…"

"…Nuts," snapped Scruffy. "You no more sound like Dunraven than Zara does."

"I won the Brisbane High's Mimicry Prize last year; I could imitate the prime minister, our top cricketer, the…"

"… This is no Christmas panto," said Caveman.

"I can use a walkie-talkie and I'm stopping Dunraven's horror show, *now.*"

Seeing his set jaw, the others reluctantly decided to let Shane have his way as he ran his finger down the list of names lining the device. He stopped at the first one he recognised; *Cartwright*: *Manager.* He took a deep breath and pressed the call button. The response was almost immediate.

"Yeah? Cartwright."

"Lord Dunraven speaking," snapped Shane.

The three friends' eyes widened; Shane's English accent really did sound like Dunraven's.

"Oh, right, er, yes, Your Lordship. What can I do for you?"

"An unexpected emergency has arisen, Cartwright. Halt all operations and transportation until further notice. I shall update you shortly. Goodbye."

Seeing the grudging admiration on his friends' faces, Shane released the breath he'd been holding. "How did I do?"

The sound of approaching footsteps and someone humming outside the main door made all four stiffen.

Shane pointed. "Hide under those heating pipes!"

He moved like a panther to position a nearby chair into place below the ceiling light, then leapt onto the seat. Stretching upwards, he deftly loosened the light bulb from its socket. As everything plunged into darkness, he repositioned the chair and in the same sweeping movement, threw himself beneath the handrail and squeezed in between Tubs and Scruffy.

The sound of codes being punched into the door lock guaranteed nobody made the slightest sound or movement.

Chapter 19

The door slid open and a squat, muscular man entered, mechanically chewing gum. Clipboard under his arm, he was lazily adjusting his earphones which gave Shane those few precious seconds to wriggle closer to the others. All were now obscured from view by the shadow cast by the wide handrail.

"That bloody fuse again," the man muttered. Having repeatedly failed to turn on the light, he flicked on his torch.

Shane watched the flashlight illuminate the man's features, accentuating the long facial scar that showed like an inky gash of paint. Head moving to the music, the man scanned the wall instruments, then stopped, his feet close to Scruffy's face.

"Schwartz, sir," he said into his walkie-talkie. "Gestation. Come in."

"I'm aware of your whereabouts, Schwartz," came the softly-spoken reply.

Dunraven!

"Still problems with No 12, sir. Raised protein and blood sugar and the pulse is all over the gaff."

"I pay you to provide accurate information, not personal opinions. What are the *precise* readings?"

"Sorry, Lord Dunraven," Schwartz grovelled. "Pulse: two hundred and five, sir. Glucose…"

"…Abort. Unplug it instantly then get a Cleansing and Sterilising Detail there immediately. How are 18 and 17?"

"Stable and normalish, sir."

"*Normalish?*"

"I, I… mean normal, sir."

"Maturity time, final batch?"

115

"Er, less than an hour, sir."

"Right on schedule. Camera 26 is suffering a periodic glitch. See to it. Organise the vans for embryo transfer to Acceleration."

"At once, sir."

"Out."

Shane heard Schwartz swear under his breath as he worked various dials and knobs until a loud gurgling sound resonated inside the darkened room. Every nerve on hyper alert, he listened as Schwartz spoke into his walkie-talkie.

"Frank, it's Bruno; Gestation. Have the vans ready for full-term embryo transfer to Acceleration. Order a Cleansing and Sterilising Unit and a replacement container – on the double. For heaven's sake check that the bleeding thing is sterile; he's on the warpath."

Humming, Schwartz replaced his earphones and sauntered out.

As the four struggled to their feet, Scruffy gasped, "Whoof; what a stench from his scummy socks."

"What about smashing the machines?" said Caveman, his fists clenched. "Maybe wreck the computers?"

"Those guards would be on us," said Tubs, "like a ton of bricks."

"While Zara's on her way," said Shane, "let's check out the final Acceleration Station."

"This was to be our last go, right?" said Scruffy, looking to the others for support.

"Scoot off if you want to, Peter, it's OK by me."

Scruffy checked the ring of lined faces. "Forget it."

No lights showed outside; the only sound was the soft sigh of the wind rustling the foliage above their heads.

116

"Ssh," Shane hissed. "Hear it?"

"What?" whispered Scruffy.

"An electrical hum. Over there somewhere."

"Shane, you could hear a bluebottle fart," sniggered Tubs, trying to jazz things up a little.

They needed something to break the tension and that was it! Despite their predicament, each involuntarily spluttered, trying to suppress the laughter as they scampered after Shane, hands across their mouths. In single file they ran through the pines towards the dark building nearby. The outside plaque read:

PHASE 4
ACCELERATION STATION
AUTHORISED PERSONNEL ONLY

Rows of empty containers lay stacked against the side of the building; a fleet of electric vans was parked nearby. Spirals of smoke drifted from the two chimneys on the roof. As they crept closer, throbs emanating from the building were making the earth vibrate beneath their feet.

"Maybe I should, er, wait for you guys outside?" faltered Tubs.

"The cops will be along any minute," said Shane.

"What's that?" said Scruffy pointing to the shadowy three-storey structure. Considerably taller and larger than the other buildings within the Complex, its darkened, all-glass penthouse suite suddenly lit up, illuminating the surrounding woods. They watched Dunraven enter, accompanied by the two Cloning Directors, each holding a long-stemmed glass.

"That's his HQ …" began Shane when a shaft of widening light arced through the darkness as the doors of the Acceleration Section began to slide open.

Immediately all four shot behind the line of trees as an electric van exited, four see-through plastic coffins in its rear compartment. A naked man lay inside each, arms folded across his chest. Each body was an exact replica of the other. Schwartz sprinted from the building and hammered his fist against the driver's window.

"Hey, brain dead," he snarled. "Every batch for Final Programming must be checked out. Understand?" Shaking his head, he hollered, "Hey, Frank, I need you to countersign for this lot."

An unshaven, white-coated figure appeared and scrawled his signature on Schwartz's clipboard.

"Frank, how do you work with these zombies? This bleeder doesn't even understand simple English."

"Have you tried German?"

Both guffawed, clapping each other on the back.

Tears of humour still in his eyes, Schwartz waved the driver onward. "Right, Fritz, take these sleeping beauties to HQ." Addressing Frank he added, "It beats me why Dunraven insists on personally programming these creatures."

"He likes to be the Big Daddy. Ever see any of the sods smile?"

"They've little to smile about; spend their first months of life in a glass case; three weeks in an Accelerator Machine, work their butts off, then kick the bucket after six months."

"Yeah."

The two men walked away, allowing Shane to examine the building's interior. "This must be where they produce the final clones," he croaked.

Stooping low, they scuttled behind the last line of vehicles as the door slid noiselessly closed behind them.

Shane raised his head and cautiously surveyed the brightly-lit building which stretched fifty metres, metal-door exits to the front and rear. Every parked vehicle carried an empty coffin with lines of wires and tubes protruding from its front and rear. To get a clearer look, Shane crept forward between the rows of vehicles.

Angled at forty-five degrees to the floor, a long column of coffins stood, each sealed by a metal-handled door. Resembling tilted glass beds, the nearest coffins were empty. Behind, a queue of vans waited, surrounded by clone guards working under Frank's command. A pair of guards lifted each sleeping body out of its container then swung the senseless being into the rear of each van. Here, two more guards took charge of the body and settled it inside the coffin which was lined with white upholstery.

"Careful," roared Frank, shaking his fist. "They're not sacks of potatoes; No's 13 to 20 are for Surgery. If one of you propeller heads drops anything, the Master will sort you out with a few hundred volts."

The clones shuffled, exchanging uneasy glances.

"Schwartz, this lot are for Programming," Frank said, consulting his worksheet. "Bring the rest over from Gestation."

As Frank decanted bottles of coloured liquids into the vertical tubes protruding from the lid of each coffin, Scruffy whispered, "What's in those bottles?"

Shane squinted as he read off the labels. "Er... vitamins, amino acids, electrolytes, carbohydrates..."

"... What's all that in aid of?" grunted Caveman.

"Dunraven must grow each embryo," whispered Tubs, "into a fully-grown adult within three weeks. That takes a lot of stuff."

"Let's go," said Shane. "We've got enough to put

119

Dunraven behind bars forever."

"Have you, indeed?" growled a nearby voice.

They whirled around. Barrel-chested Schwarz stood behind them, his face creased in a smug grin, a snub-nosed pistol pointed in their direction. Holding the weapon against Shane's cheek, he waved four clone guards forward, their blue eyes fixed, their faces expressionless.

Shane was furiously trying to get to grips with what was happening, but his mind refused to engage as Schwartz's putty-like features continued to beam with pleasure.

"Next time you impersonate Dunraven, smart ass, remember his Lordship never says hello or goodbye to anyone. And all our phones and walkie-talkies are fitted with locator devices." He addressed the waiting guards. "Hood 'em, rope 'em, take their phones and hoick 'em straight to HQ. Any backchat, chuck 'em to the meat guzzlers."

Chapter 20

The four-lay propped against the wall of the spacious, high-ceilinged suite of Dunraven's HQ's penthouse, their hands expertly bound in front with plastic rope, their feet similarly knotted. Attempting to stand upright was impossible because their ankles were loosely tied to their wrists. Above their heads, the rising moon slid filaments of eerie silver light through the shutters that barred the room's sole window. An armed clone stood on each side of the only door.

"What's goin' to happen to us?" moaned Tubs, shifting into a more comfortable position.

"At least they've taken off the hoods," said Shane.

"I could get gangrene," said Scruffy.

"Ask Kurt von Psycho to loosen your ropes," said Caveman brutally.

Shane's attention was focused on the glass orb in the centre of the room. Half the size of a football and standing on top of four marble steps, it was enclosed by a ring of purple drapes that reached to the ground. Only its opaque dome was visible. "What is *that*?" he asked.

"Some kind of church thing," said Caveman sombrely.

"Dunraven's not the religious type," said Shane. He glanced up at the ceiling, noting the painted landscapes of desolate mountain scenes, interspersed with depictions of single eyes and clusters of large boulders.

"They look like those field-trip rocks."

"They're cromlechs," answered Tubs.

"Crumlocks?"

Tubs inclined his head backwards, trying to rebalance his glasses more securely on his nose. "They're supposed to be burial grounds or places where druids prayed or..." He stopped speaking as if a particularly nasty thought had struck him.

"What about those big single eyes staring down at us?"

The uncomfortable silence was broken by Caveman. "What about those daggers then?"

All eyes swivelled to the row of wooden-handled knives hanging behind the dome, almost hidden from view. Although the blades gleamed from regular use, the handles were blackened with age.

"They remind me of the ones they use in sacrifices..." said Scruffy.

"...Leave it out," muttered Tubs uncomfortably.

Another silence fell.

"Come on, you guys," said Shane with forced cheerfulness. "Maybe Dunraven will just give us a good telling-off and send us packing?"

Although they wanted to, no one believed him. More to the point, he didn't believe it himself.

Without warning, the door slid open. A tall, thin man, immaculately suited in black, stepped regally across the threshold. The sleek black hair combed backwards and the short moustache accentuated his pallid complexion. It was the penetrating eyes, however, that immediately grabbed Shane's attention; empty and cold, making him think of deep, dark tunnels.

He didn't have to be told who it was.

Chapter 21

Dunraven laid down his phone on his antique desk, eyes sweeping the room like a falcon. "You know how I abhor inefficiency," he said, smiling bleakly at the guards. "Are the intruders absolutely secure?"

Snapping to attention, the two clones chorused, "Yes, sir."

"So, you lot ignored the signs and the dogs," continued Dunraven, addressing the group. "The first intruders were Brockenhurst's Wolf Pack..." His eyebrows arched. "So you lot must be Donnegan and Co, also of St Columbanus. Is breaking and entering part of your school curriculum?"

While his long fingers deftly worked his laptop, all lights dimmed and a wide screen lit up behind his back. Moments later, a menu appeared: *"School Personnel."* As Dunraven scrolled down, Shane recognised their names, personal details, even the names of their pets and favourite football teams.

"Was it pharmaceuticals or poison that neutralised my dogs?" purred Dunraven, his voice as friendly as a razor blade. "You Fatty, answer immediately, otherwise I'll have one of my men help you remember."

"Yes, yes, Lord Dun... rav... en," gabbled Tubs, his glasses sliding down his nose, "it was sleepin' pills."

Dunraven laid his index finger across his pursed lips. "Now, what to do with you?" he murmured.

Shane called loudly. "Hey, Dunraven, you don't scare us. The police will be along soon."

Dunraven's emotionless eyes switched to Shane. "Ah, Donnegan, isn't it? I like that; admirable characteristics in a leader; no doubt to go with your mimicry skills? Nobody knows what happens on my Estate, least of all

123

the police. Inspector McNamara, Westport's head buffoon, owes me one, so your disappearances will not merit serious investigation."

"What do you mean, disappearances?" said Tubs hoarsely.

"Tomorrow an upturned boat will be found in the estuary with some of your clothing floating nearby. This time, no bodies will be found."

"Because you're going to let us go?" said Scruffy, trying to suppress the yodel in his voice.

"Goodness gracious, no," said Dunraven. "My Venus flytraps do enjoy a little variety in their diet. Other than snacking out on dog and stray cats, they have developed a taste for live meat, rather than the same boring carcasses of Major Kurt von Konning of the Sixth Panzer Division."

A cold shiver ran down Shane's backbone as Dunraven chuckled, an entirely mirthless sound.

"But, I am impressed; nobody has ever broken through my security systems. There's also a little matter of my prize Japanese flowerbeds being smothered by somebody interfering with my sewage system, eh?" He switched off the screen, letting their photographs fizzle into the tube.

"Keep him talking," Shane whispered frantically out of the corner of his mouth. *I just wish Zara'd get her skates on.* Clearing his throat he shouted, "How did you first get the idea to clone humans, Lord Dunraven?" He hoped his question contained the required mix of reverence and admiration.

Shane knew his query was loaded; as did the others. Question was, did Dunraven?

Smoothing a crease on his lapel, Dunraven said softly, "Great men cannot explain from where their ideas originate."

Tubs took over. "But no other scientist has done what you've done, Lord Dunraven. Maybe you could get two Nobel Prizes for chemistry *and* genetics?"

"Precisely," said Dunraven, his eyes flickering. "What are a few miserable lives compared with the potential of my work? Most ailments of the kidney, eye and liver I can cure by transplantation. The problems of the body rejecting replacement organs I have overcome; the world is now entering a new, fantastic, phase."

"But isn't making humans, er, against the law?" mumbled Scruffy.

"Laws are made for the protection of fools," purred Dunraven, "not for the guidance of genius." Quickly patting the slight strands of hair that had slipped out of place, he continued. "Once upon a time, claiming the earth was round meant you were burnt at the stake. Great men like me have insufficient time to wait for legal simpletons to make up their minds."

"How did you get the liver to stop rejectin' transplanted organs?" said Tubs, blinking erratically.

Shane thought the question was screamingly artificial, but Dunraven was in too full a flow to notice.

"While other slowcoach scientists assumed the liver was responsible for rejection, I sent protein messengers to programme the brain, thereby activating the liver in whichever way I wished. That alone is worth another Nobel Prize."

Dunraven was still chuckling to himself when Caveman called out, "If you're so damned smart, why can't your clones live for longer than six months?"

A look crossed Dunraven's face, as if a dog had just fouled his best Persian carpet. "I dislike your tone, Tarpey," he said softly.

"We just don't believe you, Dunraven," said Shane, looking around at the others, mutely appealing for them to back him up. "There's no way you could do all this stuff without outside help."

Caveman, getting in on the act, shouted, "Sounds a cock-and-bull story to me."

"Rubbish," called Scruffy, his voice quaking, "in my opinion."

Shane watched as Dunraven fidgeted and rolled his thumbs against his index fingers. *That's rattled him!* Taking a deep breath Shane continued, "Try telling us the truth for a change, yeah?"

"The truth," the others chorused but Shane could hear the suppressed fear in their voices.

Dunraven rubbed the side of his face. "As this conversation will go no further than these four walls," he muttered, "there's no harm in filling you in with *all* the facts. Even my close associates remain in the dark."

He whispered something into the intercom before continuing. "I'm well aware, Master Donnegan, of why you're trying to prolong our pleasant tête-à-tête."

"What do you mean?" Shane said, feeling iciness raking his flesh. It's the cold, he told himself, knowing full well it wasn't true.

"Wasn't it your intention to keep me talking, until Miss India arrived with the police?"

The door slid noiselessly open and two clones appeared. Frogmarching a struggling, sack-covered figure between them, they deposited it at Shane's feet. Without breaking step, they saluted and withdrew.

"I think it's important that *all* members of your nosey group should be present," Dunraven said. Stepping forward he yanked off the sack with a theatrical flourish and cried, *"Abracadabra."*

On the ground lay a bedraggled Zara, securely roped, mouth bound with tape, her eyes swollen and blotched. Beside her, Snoog was whimpering, trying to cover his head with his front paws.

Chapter 22

"Are you OK?" shouted Shane, trying to struggle to his feet.

Dunraven strode forward and with his foot, slammed Shane back to the ground then dragged Zara backwards to position her against the wall beside the others. He wrenched the tape from her mouth and grabbing the dog's leash, secured the terrified animal to the radiator.

Sick with disappointment, Shane continued to stare at Zara.

"As you see," said Dunraven, smiling grimly, "both new arrivals are unharmed, although perhaps lucky to be alive. Females are best suited to kitchen activities hence Miss Singh is the first member of the opposite sex to visit my HQ."

Tears were running down Zara's face. Raw wheals marked her skin where the gagging strips had been. "Schwartz and the guards were waiting for me," she whimpered as the words tumbled out. "They put me beside the flytraps made me confess how we flooded the rose garden, put a sack over my head and said that if I made the slightest move..." Her head dropped.

Dunraven walked across to the row of daggers. Attached to each end of the long wooden rack, four knives hung by their handles in descending order of length. He unhooked the nearest and ran his finger along the blade, a strange light in his eyes.

That same incessant voice, buried somewhere in Shane's memory was repeating the same message; *remain focused; remain patient.* Through the window and out of the corner of his eye, a brief slash of silver splitting the night sky caught his attention. Before he could focus, it was gone. *A falling star! Supposed to mean good luck. Yeah.* "All five of us are here now, Dunraven," he said, with as much nonchalance as he could muster. "We're still waiting to hear the truth."

Dunraven laid down the knife. "The truth," he said vacantly, "the whole truth and nothing but the truth, so help me, Donnacha Donn."

"*Donnacha Donn?*" muttered Shane, casting a furtive look at the others.

"After an ancient burial place was discovered under Westport House," continued Dunraven, "I decided to do a little digging, *after* Professor Hughes had departed. The Fomorian druids were great magicians, in constant contact with the movements of the universe and offered sacrifices on special astronomical occasions." He paused and pointed. "You are in the presence of the greatest artefact ever given to mankind, a gift of mind-boggling power. The leader of the Fomorians was Donnacha Donn, compared with whom Merlin the Magician could only be considered a prankster. All we know about the Fomorians are spiteful tales written by ignorant Christian scribes. But the Fomorians did engrave their findings on a certain stone Tablet, discovered on that cold winter's evening. By me."

"Bu... bu... but..." stuttered Tubs, "...the druids had no written language..."

"Correct, Master McAuley; this Tablet has no words. Only symbols. I am the first man to merge the combined powers of religion and science."

Dunraven waited for his words to sink in. "This Tablet... communicates. The spirit and voice of the Donnacha Donn are locked into its symbols. Don't look so surprised; today, do we not make calculations on a microchip that would take the average man a million years to

130

carry out? The Fomorian Tablet connects me with the Great Druid wherever he resides, close by or light years away."

Dunraven paused to onehandedly smooth down the ends of his short moustache. "Science and religion are not enemies, simply two different languages telling the same story. The funding for all my work," he waved his arm in a wide circle, "rests with the Donnacha Donn. He taught me how to genetically modify plants and best of all, the secrets of transforming lead into gold — until that idiot, No 2, failed to lock the formula in my safe and misplaced it somewhere. A thousand volts failed to jog his memory. That's one of the Tablet's flaws; it will only answer a question once."

Shane's towering incredulity was being overwhelmed by the nagging feeling that Dunraven really was insane. "Are you telling me that your ideas come from an ancient cement brick?"

"These ideas are s*poken* not *written*," answered Dunraven coldly. "Aside from being a warrior race, the Fomorians were also philosophers and inventors, men who believed in doing good for humanity."

"For humanity's sake," said Caveman through clenched teeth, "you should book yourself into a lunatic asylum."

"The Fomorians," continued Dunraven pleasantly, "lived in far more *dangerous* times than your pampered lot, Mr Tarpey."

Shane's voice was hushed. "What do you mean?"

"Today is a cash-and-carry world; four thousand years ago, a different currency was used."

Dunraven's lips formed an oval shape as if he were whistling a silent tune. His well-manicured fingers tapped out a rhythm as he allowed the suspense to build.

131

"What are you talkin' about?" spluttered Tubs.

"You're the smart one, Fatty; haven't you spotted the clues?" Dunraven nodded towards the rack of knives. "The Ancients were always offered special sacrifices."

"Wha... wha... what do you mean...?" stammered Scruffy.

"You'll soon see."

Chapter 23

Dunraven's demeanour abruptly changed as he strode across to the central dome. He reminded Shane of a shark about to attack as he unhooked the white smock hanging at the foot of the marble steps and drew it over his head.

All lights dimmed, leaving only shadows on the walls and across the high-arched ceiling. The room began to glow with a strange radiance as Dunraven pulled the curtain cord to unveil the book-shaped slab of glazed stone beneath. The size of a portable radio, the surface of the smooth, grey-green object was covered with long lines of irregularly shaped hieroglyphs. Embossed along the sides were various combinations of spirals, lozenges, arcs and chevrons. None of its engravings bore any resemblance to any alphabet Shane had ever seen.

Arms outstretched, Dunraven called out, "O, Great Fomorian Druid, your most humble servant approaches in a spirit of reverence. I ask for assistance in my task of seeking a better world."

He lowered his arms then placed both hands on the slab, palms downward.

For what seemed an eternity, the ensuing silence screamed in Shane's ears. At last, a voice replied; a deep gravelly sound, that seemed to take a long time coming, as if travelling over great distances of time and space. Carrying a slight echo, the authoritative voice made Shane shiver. The words were spoken slowly and with a slight accent, as if English wasn't the speaker's first language.

"The Donnacha Donn listens," it boomed.

"Oh, Great One," called Dunraven, "my work to improve mankind is threatened by evil invaders. I request the advice of the Great Donnacha Donn."

"Your task," continued the voice in the same alien cadence, "is to improve the race of mankind. Destroy these enemies without further ado."

Shane shot a glance at the others and realised by their blank stares that they had heard nothing; only he and Dunraven could hear the Druid!

"Tomorrow marks your stellar solstice, O, Great Donnacha Donn," called Dunraven. "The most favourable time to offer a double sacrifice of convicted criminals."

The illumination within the dome slowly died and the block of stone became shrouded in darkness. Dunraven genuflected and as the room lights came on again, he removed the gown and stopped halfway down the steps. Shane saw a newer, more unsettling glint in his eyes.

"See how my work for the future is being helped by forces from the past?" he said. "The Fomorian solstice is a time for renewal, joy and celebration. Sadly, not for you."

Shane's mind was in turmoil. His friends' perplexed faces confirmed that they hadn't heard the Druid – or whatever it was – their expressions also registered that they regarded Dunraven as a lunatic. *I must be patient; I must wait for my chance.*

"Weren't you going to feed us to the flytraps, Lord Dunraven?"

"Three of you will provide the plants' breakfast; the other two will be sacrificed. You may pass your remaining hours deciding who will die in the flytraps. You, Master Tarpey, will be first to feel the cold caress of bronze." As the door slid open, he added. "Don't bother trying to escape. The sole exit can only be opened from the outside." He allowed his words to hang like a blade, then he was gone.

Overcome by a crushing sensation of doom, Shane saw his own terror mirrored in the others' eyes and the realisation hit him like an uppercut; *we've only a few hours left to live.*

Chapter 24

"I'm so *afraid,* Shane," whispered Zara tearfully.

"Me too," said Scruff.

"That nutter is wired to the moon," muttered Caveman.

"Maybe the guy is hearin' voices," said Tubs, "ramblin' on to some non-existent Druid."

"I heard the Druid," said Shane.

Four heads swivelled in his direction.

"What did you say?" croaked Zara.

"You heard me," said Shane.

Nobody broke the long silence until Zara said, "Shane, are you sure you're OK?"

Shane heard the concern in her voice but didn't reply.

"The whole thing's finally got to him," muttered Scruffy, shaking his head.

"I heard the Druid," said Shane, "as clear as if he was standing beside me. I can't explain it."

"Nobody sacrifices me," said Caveman, "without a fight."

"This whole thing was your idea, Shane, remember..." began Scruffy.

"...This is no time for blaming each other, Scruff," said Shane. "Forget that sacrifice stuff. I'm getting us out of here. We've got just one chance."

Despite their guarded expressions, he could read in their eyes the terrifying possibility that he was becoming as deranged as Dunraven. "Hey, isn't anybody listening?" he demanded.

"What's the plan then?" said Zara.

"Follow me," Shane answered, rolling over to lie face downward on the carpet. Although his hands were

137

roped to his feet, he was still able to flip himself over on his side and by carrying out half turns and rolling over barrel fashion, he quickly distanced himself from the others.

"What is he up to?" asked Tubs incredulously.

"It's my opinion that he's lost it," mumbled Scruffy.

Shane carried out some more sideways tumbles, coming to rest beneath the row of knives.

Caveman's face lit up. "He's going for the daggers!"

In a sudden flurry of activity, the others stretched themselves out on the floor and began to barrel roll after Shane. The dust attacked their noses and eyes, causing Scruffy to repeatedly sneeze.

"It's my hay fever..." he spluttered.

"...Keep moving," growled Caveman, "or you'll really need a doctor."

Shane lay beneath the weapon rack, watching the others line up close by.

"Those daggers are far too high, Shane," said Tubs, sounding crushed with disappointment. "No way could you reach them."

"I've worked it out," said Shane. "Caveman, you're the strongest, so lie on your back directly under the rack. Next, I'm going to try and stand up with my back against the wall, balance on your stomach and by shooting myself upwards, crash the top of my head against the wood. When I come back down it might be painful..."

"...But those fallin' knives will stick into you or Caveman." shouted Tubs.

"No," said Shane, "they're hanging from the end of the rack; I'm going to aim for the middle..."

138

"…Get on with it," Caveman rasped.

Eyes wide, the others watched as Caveman manoeuvred himself into position. From his propped stance close to the wall, Shane shuffled towards Caveman's prostrate body. Raising his hands and feet simultaneously, he made an ungainly hop and landed on Caveman who was unable to disguise the spasm of pain shooting across his features. Frantically trying to retain his balance, Shane toppled backwards and landed in a clumsy heap at his friend's feet. Shaking sweat from his eyes, he half hopped, half staggered upright.

"We try again," he panted.

This time he balanced carefully on Caveman's frame and after steadying himself, sprang upwards. Lacking sufficient momentum, his head again failed to contact the rack and as he came down, his knees again rammed into Caveman's ribcage, expelling the breath from his friend's lungs in a painful gasp.

"Sorry, Mike…" Shane began.

"…Anything's better than lying on that altar."

They regarded each other warily before the next attempt. Prior to Shane launching himself towards the rack, Caveman had bent his spine and tensed his back muscles that provided Shane with that extra boost of upward momentum. The top of Shane's head barely touched the wooden slat and on landing, he crunched into Caveman's chest and fell helplessly across the floor.

"Wait!" cried Zara. "Why not get Caveman to lie on his stomach? In that way he can squat on his elbows and knees and you should get much more height."

Shane breathed, "Good one, Zara."

With Caveman in this new position, Shane balanced himself with his back against the wall, his full weight bearing down on Caveman's spine. As Shane gained further control of his balance, Caveman partially raised himself on to his knees and elbows and waited. Their heavy breathing was the only sound in the room.

"On my count of three, pitch me upwards as hard as you can. Ready?"

"Less talk."

"ONE, TWO, THREE…" Such was Caveman's upward muscular thrust that Shane felt the topmost bones of his head move as he smashed against the rack. He heard the wood splinter and on descending, both knees hammered into Caveman's tortured back and Shane rolled over twice and lay still. The sound of metal striking the ground dampened his pain. Scruffy was already picking up the nearest knife with his tied hands.

"Your head's bleeding," cried Zara.

"Cut!" panted Shane, struggling into a sitting position and proffering his bound wrists to Scruffy. He shot a glance at the fractured rack, placed a handkerchief against his head and within minutes all were free, rubbing their chafed and cramped limbs. *How could I smash through three centimetres of mahogany?* "You great big lump, Mike," he said.

"Get off my back," said Caveman, managing a wan smile.

"When you're all finished congratulating yourselves," interrupted Zara, "we have a small matter of that locked door."

"There's only one way of getting out of this hellhole," said Shane slowly.

All eyes focused on Shane. Nobody dared speak.

"Take on the zombies?" ventured Caveman eventually.

"No, we'll never get out under our own steam. We need somebody else's help."

140

"Who?" the others chorused.

"The Donnacha Donn."

Chapter 25

"This whole Donnacha Donn nonsense is rigged," said Scruffy grimly. "In my opinion it's some sort of Wizard of Oz microphone setup. Other than Dunraven, you, Shane, are the only one who heard this druid."

"If it wasn't for Shane," snapped Zara, "we'd still be in knots."

Caveman cut in. "Let's take our chances with the knives."

"Shane talking to this Druid guy is our only chance," put in Zara fiercely.

"Those clones are all brawn and muscle," said Shane. "No way can we take them on. I reckon that this Donnacha Donn, or whatever he is, has been tricked by Dunraven – I heard him say that Dunraven was doing good for the world – *good!*"

"No one's going to sacrifice me," said Caveman, punching his fist into his palm.

Shane held up his hand. "I bet the Druid doesn't know what really ticks with Dunraven. Making contact with him is our only chance. But it's risky."

"What do you mean, risky?" said Tubs, biting his lip.

"If this Donnacha guy," said Shane, "doesn't believe us then he might do, well, anything…" He fell silent.

"Look," said Caveman pointing, "spears."

Close to the central dome, partly hidden by another purple drape, a row of wooden-handled spears hung, suspended by thongs inserted into the end of each shaft. Caveman strode across and unhooked two, tested their balance then ran his thumb over the bronze tips.

"This one's mine," he muttered with grim

satisfaction.

He handed the other to Shane, drew back his arm and launched the weapon with all his strength at the wooden fireplace. Two seconds later, Shane drove his weapon at the same target.

Caveman strolled over and levered the tip of his weapon free. Unable to remove the second spear, he shot Shane a puzzled look. "Where do you get the strength?" he muttered.

"Spears versus guns," interrupted Zara. "I wonder who'd win?"

"Enough talking," said Shane, freeing Dunraven's robe and sliding inside.

"I hope you know what you're doing, Shane," Zara whispered.

I wish I did. Only two people heard the Druid; Dunraven's barmy; does that mean I'm the same? "Let's do it," he said in the flat clipped tone of a man of action but he felt his legs tremble.

No one spoke as Shane approached the Fomorian Tablet. Without warning, the air around the altar began to radiate and pulsate with a bright reddish glow that was suffused with vague bluish tinges. With shaking hands he lifted the lid of the dome, uncovered the Tablet and bowed. The room was now in darkness, the silence total. He noted that a distant corner of the room was glowing in a shaft of moonbeam.

Shane knelt and placed his hands exactly as Dunraven had done. The stone felt cool, heavy with history. Every cell in his body felt electrified; he barely recognised his own quaking voice; "Oh, Great Donnacha Donn, a faithful servant approaches… er…" he faltered.

"*In a spirit of reverence…*" prompted Tubs from behind.

144

"… In a spirit of reverence," Shane mumbled before struggling through a repeat of Dunraven's address.

For twenty long seconds, all he could hear was his thumping heart. Suddenly a thunderous voice sounded, seeming to come from somewhere close by.

"Who DARES address the Donnacha Donn?"

A wave of ice-cold dread washed over Shane as he fought for words. *I cannot believe that whoever is talking to me is supposedly dead for thousands of years. My tongue feels like a sponge…* "Me and my friends," came his strangled reply, "are in great danger. We are prisoners of an evil man who's going to kill us. Because I know you are a great Fomorian druid, I ask for your help."

"Who threatens the life of one of tender years?" boomed the voice.

"Lord Dunraven."

"Dunraven? A man of evil?"

Shane swallowed hard, trying to control his tottering thoughts. *I need the toilet.* "I'm telling the truth," he blurted.

"Lay your hands on the altar," commanded the voice.

His insides churning like a spin dryer, Shane wiped his moist palms on Dunraven's shroud before grasping the stone. As his fingertips engaged the shapes and indentations on the Tablet's surface, he fought an overwhelming sense of awe and fear, knowing that despite everything he thought he knew about life, he was now standing where the worlds of history and myth intermingled. He felt a series of hot, then cold waves leap along his fingers then shoot through his quaking body before exiting through the soles of his trainers. The light emanating from the stone began to increase to such intensity that he had to shield his eyes from the radiance.

145

"Your words ring of the truth." This time the voice was friendly. A long pause followed. "You are Shay-An, are you not?"

Shane shot bolt upright as if someone had pierced him with a sharp nail. *How does this thing know me? I never mentioned my name, so how…?*

The Druid's voice cut in. "We have already met. I was your guide around Westport House."

"My guide?" gasped Shane, his mind unable to absorb further thunderbolts. "You mean you're Don? The guy with the beard and the cloak?"

"Donn," corrected the voice, "that's two Ns, not one. I am the Donnacha *Donn*."

Shane thought he heard a chuckle. A three-thousand-year-old sound? *What is happening?*

"Each stellar solstice," said the Donnacha Donn, "and on other occasions, I and other Fomorians, return to what remains of our ancient Temple."

"But why was only I able to see you? Why can't my friends hear you? I think I'm going mad." Bewildered, he swung around. The others were staring open mouthed at him, their faces contorted by disbelief. *They're finally convinced I've gone barmy…*

As Shane shook his head to clear his thoughts, the Druid continued. "My son, there is much to learn about who you are. Remember how much you recollected about the past when walking around Westport House?"

Shane rubbed his moist forehead "Yeah," he said softly, "I could recall things from the past that I didn't think I even knew; my friend Tubs thought I was crackers." *This whole thing is crackers. Even more so, because this guy and me have similar sounding names; Donn… Donnegan…*

"Explain, Shay-An, how I have been deceived by

Dunraven."

Shane inhaled deeply then briefly described all that had happened since he'd first entered the Westport House Estate, becoming more relaxed the longer he spoke.

When he'd finished, another silence followed before the Donnacha boomed, "The Fomorian Tablet must only be used for the good of mankind. I have been tricked. My wrath is great."

As the light slowly faded, Shane continued to stare spellbound at the Tablet, trying unsuccessfully to glean some sort of meaning from its signs and hieroglyphs. He realised he was alone; alone with his thoughts, alone with the realisation that only he could communicate with this mind-boggling person or thing; alone in trying to figure out just why he felt such a bizarre bond between himself and the Donn...

Forget everything; concentrate on getting us out of this hell.

As he climbed down from the altar, Shane was super conscious of his friends' fear-racked faces. As Zara helped remove the gown, the others watched uneasily, aware that during Shane's five minutes inside the dome, they had witnessed various expressions of incredulity, horror and terror sear across his face. He could read the look in their eyes – *they think I'm as mad as Dunraven!* He felt Zara's hand on his shoulder. "You OK, Shane?"

"Yeah," he nodded, his trembling fingers revealing the lie.

"All we could see," she continued, "was you talking to yourself."

"Like a fruit-and-nut case," added Tubs.

Shane stared through the window, aware that the starry dark was now tinted with gold. Using only short, terse sentences, he ran through all that had taken place inside the dome.

"Are you trying to tell us," cried Scruffy, trying to keep his voice steady, "that you've been talking to someone who's been dead for yonks?"

"Is the Druid guy goin' to help us?"

"I don't know," Shane answered in a faraway voice.

Shaking his head with that suddenness one finds in people with something serious on their minds, he added, "Let's retie ourselves so Dunraven'll think we're still prisoners."

Ensuring the knots looked convincing but with enough slackness to pull free when required, Shane loosely retied their ropes. As they adjusted to their new positions against the wall, Snoog's low growl froze their blood.

"He's back already," gasped Zara.

Chapter 26

Shane held his breath as Dunraven swished into the room in a flowing purple habit; a half-mask covered his scalp, ears and nose. Head bowed, his hands were joined in prayer and he looked neither left nor right. Imprinted on the back of his robe was a large eye, set against a background of stars and planets. Two clones marched behind, each carrying a tray, on which a dagger and a bowl of steaming oil lay.

"Place the linen and lotion as usual," said Dunraven. "Implements fully sharpened, No 3?"

"Yessir."

"Hazel-handled originals?"

"Yessir."

"Sacrificial Prayers, No 7?"

As No 7 handed over a printed sheet, Dunraven said, "A double sacrifice, so no cock-ups like last solstice; understood, No 3?"

No 3 stood rigid like a soldier under intense inspection. "Cracked handle not my fault, sir."

Dunraven took a sharp intake of breath. "Take No 3 to the Electrical Correction Unit."

Shane could see tears in No 3's eyes as he was frogmarched away, shouting, "Please, Daddy, it was an accident."

"Out," said Dunraven with chilling softness.

"They have real feelings, Caveman," whispered Shane out of the corner of his mouth.

"Forget them, Shane," said Scruffy. "What about us?"

"Will the second sacrificial victim identify itself?" said Dunraven.

"Me," said Shane.

"Always leading from the front," Dunraven said in mock admiration. "Splendid qualities."

No 7 jerked Shane away from the wall and dragged him by the back of his collar to the altar. Dunraven gripped Shane's feet and slung him onto the slab as if he were a sack of lettuce. Smiling pleasantly, he called over his shoulder. "The brute next."

Dunraven and No 7 similarly laid Caveman on the second block.

"What's keeping your Druid, Shane?" said Caveman hoarsely.

"No talking or I will cut both your tongues out," said Dunraven conversationally, regarding them as if they were cod in a fishmonger's window.

Sweat was now sticking Shane's shirt to the underlying sheet. Despite the almost overwhelming urge to sink his fingers into Dunraven's throat, he knew it would be futile. *Yesterday I was drinking milkshakes and laughing, now our lives depend on some supposedly long-dead Druid. Be patient; like that heron…*

"Don't kill Shane, Lord Dunraven," screamed Tubs. "We didn't mean any harm and we promise that…"

"… Gag them."

No 7 plucked a roll from his belt and expertly taped Tubs, Zara and Scruffy's mouths. "The others, sir?"

"I think these two can face meeting their ends unaided. Am I right, Master Donnegan?"

Shane stared unblinkingly into Dunraven's eyes without replying.

"Murdering scum," shouted Caveman, spitting in Dunraven's direction. A small splotch of saliva landed on the robe.

Shane saw Dunraven's black eyes flash but when he spoke, Dunraven's tone was measured. "Master

Donnegan will die swiftly; I will personally see to it that you, Master Tarpey, will take considerably longer."

Shane's voice was hoarse. "How come druids need human sacrifices?"

"Hush," said Dunraven, slapping Shane across the face. His tongue flicked across his lips as he unlatched the dome.

The room darkened.

With his arms spread wide, Dunraven's incantation began. "O Great Donnacha Donn, your humble servant approaches to present not one, but two sacrifices."

During the ensuing silence, Shane imagined he could hear the Donnacha's words making their way from an even greater distance than previously. He could hear the suppressed venom in the resounding voice.

"The Donnacha thanks his humble servant. Who are the sacrifices?"

Shane listened with macabre fascination to Dunraven's reply. "Er, two sinners whose, er, lives are offered to you, Donnacha Donn, Great Leader of the Fomorians."

"Names?"

"Names, O Great One?"

"NAMES!"

"Forgive me, O Great One, their names are, er, Donnegan and Tarpey."

"Crimes?"

"Lying, cheating, robbery."

"Lying and cheating are crimes punishable by death, are they not, Lord Dunraven?"

"Absolutely, Great Donnacha."

Shane could see that Dunraven was becoming more troubled and unsure as he grasped the knife and faced the Fomorian Tablet.

"No 7," called Dunraven, "spread the sacrificial

oils on the victim's chest."

Holding the dagger high above Shane's body, he began to recite something in a language Shane couldn't understand while the guard applied unpleasant-smelling lotions across his torso. He felt a droplet of Dunraven's sweat fall on his face.

"Accept this sacrifice, O Great One."

As if he had been teleported back into his recurrent nightmare, Shane hypnotically watched Dunraven raise the weapon. He wanted to scream, to roll off the altar and take his chances but terror had paralysed his limbs. And his brain.

"STOP!"

The Donnacha's thunderous order not only made Shane start; it also made Dunraven drop the knife. "The penalty for lying to the Donnacha is death." The voice simmered with rage.

His face ashen, Dunraven was blinking erratically. He looked like a man desperately searching for an out. Any out. "Yes, O Great Donnacha," he grovelled, his insect-like eyes flashing fear.

"YOU have lied to ME, Dunraven." The Donnacha's voice had dropped to a purr.

"There must be some mistake, O Great One."

Seeing Dunraven's demeanour crumbling, Shane was reminded of the heron's beak spearing through the surface of the river, impaling its prey…

"No mistake," said the Druid.

A new sound caught Shane's attention, a prolonged hiss – Dunraven's laptop was surrounded by a circle of tiny flames, a strange purple colour, slowly licking upwards.

The Donnacha's voice resounded again. "Master Donnegan and friends will arise and leave. Everything I helped you with, Dunraven, will burn. Witness your works tumbling around your ears."

A thunderous banging on the door was accompanied by Schwartz's shouts. "Sir! Someone has set fire to the place! Get out before it's too late."

Shane had already thrown his ropes aside and was tearing tapes from the others' mouths. Loud whooshing noises made him whip around to see dancing bundles of fast-moving flames attack the surrounding paintings and drapes. He blinked as a loud crackle sounded close by; Dunraven was standing immobile amid a rising pillar of flame, as if held in place by some irresistible force. The hem of his gown had caught fire and as the flames danced eagerly upwards, his horror-filled eyes widened as the full realisation of his fate hit home. His face contorted, Dunraven's mouth stretched to its fullest extent as if he was screaming, but Shane could hear no sound. He grabbed No 7. "Get out. Save yourself!"

"What about my daddy?" No 7 demanded.

"He's not your daddy," shouted Shane. "Run!"

"This building is doomed, Shay-An," came the Donnacha's shout above the tumult. "Leave."

As Shane stood undecided, a loud whoosh sounded and a blazing curtain rail fell to the ground nearby.

"The roof's on fire," Zara screamed.

Shane hollered, "Grab Dunraven's mobile from the desk, Zara. Then get out! Now!"

As one, they sprinted for the exit. Scruffy was first to the door. "Oh, no!" he shrieked. "It's locked."

Chapter 27

Shane unceremoniously shouldered Scruffy aside. "Clear the doorway!" To the two bewildered clones he gasped, "Have you guys got a key?"

Both shook their heads.

"What are you doing, Shane?" screamed Zara.

"Stand aside."

Transfixed, the others watched Shane take three backward steps, drop his shoulder then plunge towards the double doors at full lick. He smashed into the wooden framework, sending it crashing into the outside passage as if it were no more than a sheet of cardboard.

Without giving what they'd seen a second thought, the others fled after Shane into the corridor which was rapidly filling with swirling smoke.

"Which way?" cried Zara, her voice unrecognisably shrill.

Shane was already halfway down the hallway. "Follow me," he hollered over his shoulder.

To the sounds of crackling wood, they rounded the end of the passageway and there ahead, through the blackening smog, they could just about recognise the main stairway.

"We've forgotten Snoog!" Shane shouted, coming to an immediate halt.

"Nobody is going back for a dog," snarled Scruffy.

"He's probably dead by now," said Zara, using both arms to push Shane forward.

"I'll get him," shouted Shane. *Snoog has all the evidence in his collar and I can't let poor Mrs Durcan spend her days watching TV by herself.* "I'll catch you up," he added and tearing back along the landing,

155

vanished into the smoke.

As the others stared helplessly at each other, a blazing beam fell from the ceiling.

Scruffy shouted, "Do what he says!"

"We can't leave Shane!" hollered Zara.

"He knows what he's doin'," said Tubs. "He's Shane, remember?"

"'Come *on!*" cried Caveman, wrenching Zara and Tubs onward.

They rattled down the stairs, taking two, sometimes three steps at a time. From all around thundered the sound of collapsing walls and the cracking of the penthouse roof; somewhere in the distance, more loud crashes were rattling the building. The noise was terrifying.

"Don't anyone fall behind!" panted Caveman.

As they reached the next floor, a door burst open and three clones tumbled out, flailing against each other. From the other side of the passageway a door shot open and another clone appeared, hands over his head, coughing and spluttering. Running forward, he blindly flung himself headlong through the nearest window, his scream lost in the turmoil.

Caveman was still leading the way when the nearside wall of Dunraven's HQ peeled away with a splintering roar. They stood petrified, waiting for the smoke to clear, disorientated by the proximity of trees and the blast of cool air on their faces. The peaceful countryside and the dawn sky made their predicament all the more appalling – twenty metres above ground was too high for them to even think about jumping.

Their eyes were dragged upwards by the harrowing new sound from the room overhead as its floorboards tilted precariously, leaning and bending in the open air. A bed teetered on the edge of the swaying floor before spiralling towards the ground. In quick succession, more beds on well-oiled wheels accelerated across the sloping room and cascaded over the lip, scattering bedclothes and mattresses into the waiting flames.

"Run," screamed Zara, "this floor's next."

On reaching the end of the stairway, the heat was becoming unbearable while the ground floor was an impassable, blazing inferno. From the crackling ground timbers, clouds of sparks were shooting high into the air, while from above, flaming chips and blobs of burning wood sap fell like melting snow.

"No way through," gasped Caveman, using his jacket to shield his face.

"Let's go back to the first floor," shouted Zara above the tumult. "Maybe we can climb out?"

Turning to remount the stairs, a shuddering crash marked where the ceiling of the first-floor hallway had disintegrated, obliterating the stairway.

"We're done," muttered Caveman through clenched teeth.

There was no way out, just an arena of all-consuming fire.

Then something remarkable occurred. The flames parted and a passageway appeared – two metres wide – as if a massive garden roller had levelled a smooth footpath through the holocaust. Tall flames raged on both sides of the aisle which led directly to the main exit some twenty metres away.

"Follow me," shouted Caveman.

Heads down, the others followed at full tilt, feeling the pungent gases attack their eyes and the backs of their throats, making them cough and weep at the same time. They shot through the main doors, faces angled upward, gratefully gulping down lungfuls of morning air, relishing that they had finally made it.

When they had put sufficient distance between themselves and the conflagration, they flopped down on the grass. For half an hour they waited, gazing in wonderment as the flames arced over Dunraven's HQ and his industrial estate, consuming everything in their path. They were barely aware of the arriving police cars and ambulances. The fire engines were last to arrive but the flames, like giant red sails in an erratic wind, only seemed to taunt the puny arcs of water from the firemen's hoses.

Unexpectedly, the thumping of helicopter blades sounded as the military craft cut in low over the trees, hovering above the lawns, sending the surrounding foliage crazy. Uniformed men wearing infrared goggles leapt down and spreading out quickly, began to methodically sweep the complex.

As the four became aware of their singed clothes and blistered faces smeared in soot, Scruffy broke the silence. "How come those flames divided to let us through?" he said. Their bloodshot eyes regarded each other as the question hovered.

"I'm sure someone was waving us forward from the main door," said Zara. She looked Caveman up and down. "You look like you've been cleaning chimneys."

"You're some picture postcard yourself, Zara."

"Wonder what's keepin' Shane?" mumbled Tubs for the umpteenth time, wringing his hands.

"Just *look* at my Gucci's..." Scruffy's voice tailed off as more crashes reverberated, sending further showers of giant sparks skyward. "At least Westport House wasn't affected."

"Poor Shane; no way could he have survived that," whispered Tubs, rubbing the heels of his hands into the corners of his eyes.

Caveman stood up. "We've waited long enough."

Aware of the cloying stench of burning rubber and charred wood, they trudged towards the main exit of the Estate. Smoke drifted between the trees, filtering and changing the rays of early sunshine to light blue. Bodies of clones lay scattered around; all appeared undamaged but their eyes were opaque and lifeless.

"Poor things," muttered Zara.

In silence they traipsed past the smouldering remnants of Dunraven's various buildings and the burnt-out shells of his fleet of electric vehicles. Scorched fields containing tall, black crisps marked where the flytraps once stood. Somewhere in the background came the banshee wails of more sirens.

Tubs choked back a sob. "Poor Shane," he repeated. "He was so brave to go back."

"Incredibly stupid, in my opinion."

"Bloody fool," muttered Caveman, blowing into his handkerchief.

"He'd more guts than the lot of you put together," cried Zara, her voice bubbling like boiling lava.

Chapter 28

Head down, Shane battled through the smoke and heat to get back into the altar room. Still tied to the radiator, Snoog was half-crazed with fear as Shane unknotted the leash before he heard the doorway collapse behind him in a mass of flaming timbers.

He was trapped.

I was mad to come back...

Through the swirling chaos, he could just about make out the hazy figure of the Donn, gesticulating and pointing furiously to the bulky fireplace on the far side of the room. With Snoog under his arm, Shane reached the featureless structure in three strides but could see nothing of consequence other than the large doorbell on the mantelpiece. In desperation more than hope, he pressed the buzzer. With excruciating slowness, two wide doors – camouflaged as bookshelves – slid open in the adjoining wall, revealing a downward flight of stairs to the left; an elevator filled with hospital trollies to the right.

Is this is one of Dunraven's escape routes?

He turned to wave his thanks but the Donn had disappeared. Shane never saw him again.

Deciding the elevator was too risky an option, he took the carpeted, air-conditioned stairway and after descending two flights, halted on a wide platform with the overhead sign:

PHASE 5
SURGERY
STAFF ONLY

"The last piece of the jigsaw," he muttered, stepping off the platform. He passed another row of medical

161

trollies to enter a compact but empty hospital ward containing eight beds. To the side, a corridor led to a long, fully-equipped but similarly deserted operating theatre.

So, his HQ is where Dunraven carries out the final phase of his evil work.

Although his nerves were on a razor's edge and he was fearful of bumping into another human being, he felt an inexplicable, furious rage sweeping through his body, expanding his ribcage. His mind was becoming overwhelmed by a kaleidoscope of fleeting visions of dying clones, Dunraven's face, corpse-filled wheelbarrows… He shook his head vigorously, trying to clear his brain but the images persisted, growing in intensity. Simultaneously he felt a surge of power sweep into his limbs and chest, causing his muscles to swell and bulge in a way he'd never experienced before. As the mysterious fury peaked and passed, his rapidly pumping heart slowed, his fists unclenched and despite still being swamped by bewildering, inexplicable anger, his outward demeanour remained calm, almost relaxed.

"I am ready," he heard himself murmur. *Ready for what?* he asked himself.

As he pondered his next move, three men hurriedly exited the nearby office. The first was a burly security guard, sporting numerous tattoos, a nose ring and exuding maximum unfriendliness. Behind him, deep in conversation, strode Dunraven's Directors of Cloning, Claude and Harry, each laden with documents. Seeing Shane, all three halted, their eyes widening while he continued to smilingly amble forward.

"Who the bloody hell…" began the guard, fumbling to free the baton hanging from his belt.

Without a word, Shane sprung forward and crashed his right, then his left fist into the man's face.

162

Toppling backwards against the wall, the guard pressed a hand over his split lips and broken nose then slid to the floor. As Shane picked up the baton, both flabbergasted directors dropped their paperwork and Harry decided to make a run for it. Expecting the move, Shane lunged, and his right foot shot between the man's legs, sending him skidding along the corridor on his back. His head thudded against the theatre door and he lay still, groaning.

Claude had decided enough was enough and attempted to wrench something from his pocket. Whether a gun or some other weapon, Shane never found out. He had already leapt into the air, his body almost horizontal to the ground as he deftly delivered a flying karate kick to Claude's temple and the director dropped to the floor without a sound.

Shane massaged his throbbing knuckles while coldly surveying the grounded trio and the corridor littered with papers. He approached the security guard who had propped himself against the wall, holding a bloodied handkerchief to his face. He grabbed the man by the back of his collar and dragged him on his knees into the middle of the corridor.

"Which is the quickest way out?" he asked conversationally, twirling the baton with his free hand.

The guard cried, "Don't hit me again; the emergency tunnel's the only way; in the basement."

Shane smiled. "You'd better be telling me the truth; if not…"

"I swear on my mother's grave."

"Get yourself and those other pigs out of my sight."

Shane waited until the three had begun stumbling along the corridor before haring back to the stairway, Snoog at his heels.

On reaching the basement, he stepped into a brightly-lit enclosure that resembled an underground car-park, lined by garage-sized units. He read off the signs – *Electrical Correction, Mortuary, Maintenance, Cryogenics* – then saw the two petrol pumps beside a fleet of Land Rovers. He successfully fought down the urge to douse the place with petrol and torch everything in sight. On checking out the *Electrical Correction Unit,* he saw two clones hunched and alone at a table. He recognised them by the numbers on their shoulder pads; No 3 and No 7. They immediately jumped to their feet and ran to shake his hand.

They're treating me like some long-lost friend... "Dunraven is gone, guys," he said. "No more electric shocks."

"Thank you, Mr Shane," they gushed.

Shane pointed to No 3. "You're no longer a number. I'm calling you, er, Dieter and you're… Wolfgang."

"Pleased-to-meet-you, Wolfgang," said Dieter, solemnly shaking hands with his companion.

"How-do-you-do, Dieter?" said Wolfgang.

"Are any other of your, er, friends left alive?" said Shane.

As Wolfgang shook his head, Dieter said, "Smoke kill all, very bad."

"Let's go."

On the way out Shane unhooked an empty back-pack from the wall, took a flash lamp and the packet of Hobnobs from the table and stuffed them inside. The illuminated sign at the end of the block showed the way: EXIT – EMERGENCY USE ONLY.

"Safety," he breathed. "At long last."

***

After three hundred metres, as the passageway opened into another grim maze of honeycombed caves, Shane realised that the exit was rarely, if ever, used. He ground his back teeth together. *That uniformed swine sent me the wrong way. No choice but to take my chances and continue forward...*

After two hours traipsing along rocky cul-de-sacs and wandering through dark tunnels, Shane had to admit he was lost. He was also cold and hungry, having already shared the last of the Hobnobs with Dieter, Wolfgang and Snoog.

I felt a draught on my cheek!

He picked up a stick, pulled a tissue from his pocket, tore off a strip and impaled it on top of the long twig. Hardly breathing, he drove it into the ground and stood, watching intently. After five seconds, the tapered end of the tissue quivered slightly then fluttered.

"Whatever puff of wind there is," he needlessly explained to Dieter and Wolfgang, "must be coming from, er, that direction." He felt his spirits rise.

With trembling fingers he removed the twig, ran fifty metres downhill, re-inserted it into the gravel and waited. The tissue again indicated the presence of wind. After repeating the procedure further along the passage, his heart sank; this time no movement came from the tissue, despite his changing its position many times. Setting down his backpack, he sat on a nearby boulder, head in hands. Snoog whimpered and feeling the animal's nose against his hand, Shane scratched the bobbing ears. "Good boy," he muttered off-handedly.

Snoog barked then pulled the bottom of Shane's jeans with his teeth. He yanked again, more vigorously this time, its tail wagging furiously.

Shane blinked then sprang upright as the full

realisation hit him. *He's telling me he knows the way home to Mrs Durcan's! And his supper.*

"Take us home, Snoog," he shouted.

The dog yelped and shot forward – leading the trio in the opposite direction to that previously envisaged by Shane!

Fifteen minutes later, Shane almost shouted with relief as he recognised the Professor's AMSs in the distance. Snoog was sniffing inquisitively around a wooden-handled dagger lying on the ground. Fresh questions were exploding inside Shane's brain. *Who carries ancient daggers around here? This one must belong to those guys whose DNA comes from the Bronze Age. Or from Ancient Greece...*

"Good boy, Snoog. Lead the way."

Chapter 29

Mr Stubbs rechecked the time. 7.10 am.

"This cannot be happening," he repeated, rising from his chair. His wide eyes shot from one haggard face to the next. "A pupil under my care missing... cloning human beings... it's unbelievable... I mean..."

Bewildered, he looked around the chalet, sat down, surveyed the four then stood up again. "So you haven't been to the police station or... have some more tea..." He rummaged for his phone in his pyjamas. "I must inform the... the headmaster... how am I going to explain to Shane's father and mother... I mean his aunt and uncle... Why didn't you call me?"

"We had no way of contacting anyone," said Zara wearily, "until I grabbed Dunraven's phone."

Mr Stubbs glanced at his watch. "You lot are all in. Off to bed – now. We'll meet at *The Helm*; afternoon sometime? You'll feel much better after a decent sleep..." He rested his hand across his forehead. "Poor Shane... are you sure?"

Caveman scowled. "We waited forever."

"Off you go... I'll look after everything. Are you sure you're OK, Zara?"

"I'm *ecstatic,* sir," she said, making no attempt to disguise the heavy sarcasm.

Caveman looked at his watch and made for the door. "See you all later at *The Helm* then."

"Where's he sneaking off to?" said Zara.

"His dad's developed dementia so Caveman gets the farm up and runnin' before school; same in the evenin'."

"Every day?" said Zara, frowning.

"Twenty-four-seven," said Scruffy.

Zara clasped her throat with her hand. "But... but nobody ever told me," she whispered.

"You never asked."

Zara ran to the open door. "Wait, Michael," she cried. "You just can't go home without breakfast; you need to eat something after all that... you know."

Caveman stared at his feet without moving before slowly turning around. "Thanks," he muttered. As their eyes met, he added, "Appreciated, Zara."

"Food before sleep," said Tubs, pushing past. "I could eat the head off a horse."

***

Approaching *The Helm,* the four friends realised it was a buzzing hive of conversation and activity, despite the early hour. An RTE news van squatted on Westport quay while groups of people stood on the pavement, talking animatedly. Surrounded by onlookers, two police cars and an ambulance were parked outside the main gates of Westport House. In the distance, partially blocking the sun, an ominous black cloud hung over the ruins of Dunraven's industrial complex.

The smell of a morning fry-up drifting from *The Helm* made the four realise just how long it had been since they'd even seen food.

"Breakfasts are on me," said Scruffy.

"Is Tight Fist puttin' his hand in his pocket?" said Tubs in mock amazement.

"The flames must've loosened his purse strings..." began Zara but she didn't finish the sentence.

A stunned silence fell as they recognised the three figures proceeding towards them along Westport harbour. They felt like rubbing their eyes but there could be no doubt – a dishevelled, sooty-faced Shane was approaching, holding two clones by their hands, Snoog ambling ahead. For that split second, the friends stood still, staring at each other in disbelief, then rushed forwards, hugging, pummelling, launching questions and laughing, all at the same time. Their joy was so infectious that a nearby couple began videoing the encounter on their phones. As Shane introduced Dieter and Wolfgang to the others, Dishcloth appeared in *The Helm's* doorway and yelled, "What's keeping you lot? Breakfast is ready."

As they entered the café, Dishcloth clapped Shane on the shoulder. "The police have already nabbed someone called Schwartz and his cronies on their way to Knock Airport with a load of funny merchandise..."

"... Any word of Dunraven?" interrupted Shane.

"The police reckon," continued Dishcloth, "that the charred body in the HQ is his. An accidental electrical fire, by all accounts. No more reported casualties other than all the clones; smoke inhalation it seems. I'm told Professor Hughes will run Westport House from now on."

As everyone around the table began to jabber and interrogate each other, Shane raised his hands. "Oi! Let's eat first then I'll explain everything later in the downstairs annexe. Hey, Dishcloth, I told Dieter and Wolfgang you might have jobs for them? They're happy to sign a six-month contract then see how things go after that. OK, guys?"

Without the slightest hint of embarrassment, the pair stood up and hugged each other. "Thank you, Mr Shane," said Dieter, "for us not being burnt dead."

Wolfgang smiled. "See, Mr Shane, we can now speak England very best, yes?"

Shane whispered to Zara, "Maybe they'll live

normal lives if they're treated properly and get good food and…"

"… Did someone say food?" Tubs butted in.

Dishcloth elbowed Shane and pointed. "Someone over there is *particularly* anxious to speak to you."

Chapter 30

An unreadable expression on his face, Professor Hughes was sitting alone at the corner table and waved Shane over.

"So, you are not dead after all?" he said with exaggerated seriousness, but Shane could see crinkles of humour around his eyes. "You and your friends' exploits are all over the TV and I hear you're to receive a special commendation from the President."

"I've a lot to tell you, sir."

"I'm beginning to suspect," said the Professor, leaning back in his chair, "that you know far more about these Fomorians than you've been telling me; correct?"

Shane didn't reply but instead began a craftily censored version of his exploits on the Estate while the Professor gazed through the window at the distant shape of Clare Island. Shane ended his account by dramatically dropping the dagger on the table. "I found that beside your AMSs."

The Professor shot upright and scrutinised the knife. "Fomorian," he said eventually. "Have you examined this weapon?"

"No, Professor, I just popped it in my backpack and..."

"... Its grip is unusually wide, suggesting that the owner was inordinately big and strong." He took the weapon closer to the window. "The top of handle has been carved into the shape of a large eye. Hmm, the only people using eyes as such were the Ancient Egyptians in their devotion to the Eye of Horus..."

"... What about the one-eyed Cyclopes?" interrupted Shane, itching to impress the Professor.

"... I'm talking about *real* people, Shane, not

Greek fairy tales. Somebody lost this weapon after you and I visited the AMSs; it certainly wasn't dropped off by spaceship."

I was expecting him to laugh at his own joke but he didn't even smile.

"This knife has also been used recently," the Professor continued, scratching his earlobe. "Are you sure none of your friends heard or saw this Donnacha Donn?"

"Absolutely."

"So, other than Lord Dunraven, only you were privy to the Donn's exchanges?"

"Er, yes, Professor."

"Neither can I comprehend how a teenager can smash mahogany shelves and knock fully-grown men about." He set the dagger down. "When you first met this Donnacha chap, what did he say?"

"He said he was a guide and…"

"… His *exact* words."

"Well, I *think* he said he was a guide… no, wait…" Shane rubbed his furrowed forehead. "He might have said that he was… a Watcher… yes… that was the word he used. But that doesn't make sense; watching what? Anyway, any news about the box from the crypt, Professor?"

"Our tests could only conclude that it was used to house some valuable or religious artefact." He handed Shane a sheet of paper. "These are copies of the symbols adorning the box."

Shane's eyes widened as he stared at the drawings.

"Shane? What's the matter?"

"I… recognise… these," he said slowly.

"From where, in heaven's name?"

"There're the same signs that were on the

Fomorian Tablet, you know, when I first contacted the Donn back in the HQ."

"That crypt must be an important Fomorian site," said the Professor, clicking his fingers. "But how did you locate such a well concealed place? The team and I missed it entirely."

"Lucky accident, sir."

The Professor shot a quizzical look at Shane "Umm, maybe we are getting closer to unlocking our ancestors' mysterious history."

If I don't get back soon, Tubs will have handed over all those sausages to history... Deftly changing the subject, he said cheerfully, "Is it true that you'll be the new man in charge of Westport House, Professor?"

"Yes, yes, indeed. The House will shortly reopen to the public. I see your friends are getting restless, Shane. You and I have *much* to discuss later. Would you be happy to donate the dagger, and the box you found, to my new Fomorian Section of the Westport House museum?"

"No probs, Professor."

***

In the downstairs annexe, Dishcloth laid down a loaded tray. "There's your milkshakes and a tray of Mrs Durcan's freshly-baked cupcakes. Big fires are great for business. Dieter and Wolfgang sure know how to work; that pair never stop. And by the way, the Army boys nabbed those two cloning directors. I'll say nothing about you lot losing my camera – all in a good cause, eh?"

As the door closed behind Dishcloth, all eyes swivelled to Shane.

"Face it, Shane," Zara began, resting her chin in

her palm. "There's something weird about you. Come on, you must have noticed it?"

The ensuing silence was broken by Shane. "Maybe I am a bit different," he admitted. "So what? Isn't everybody? I can't paint like you, Zara, or make electrical gadgets like Finbar..." As he spoke, he slyly lifted a cake and laughingly lobbed it across the table at Caveman. "Nobody can plough a field like Mike Tarpey," he cried and launching another cake at Scruffy, added, "Or squirrel away money like Peter Woods, yeah?"

Caveman and Scruffy promptly retaliated by zooming cakes at Shane; Zara and Tubs joined in the missile interchange until all Mrs Durcan's ammunition was eventually used up. Shane was smiling, knowing that behind the raucous laughter and devil-may-care horseplay, his friends were exulting in the joy of just being back in one piece. As Snoog foraged under the table for cake remnants, Shane struck the table with his fist.

"Oi! Does anyone want to hear about what happened after I went back for Snoog?"

"Begin at the moment you left us in the HQ," said Scruffy.

"Down to the smallest detail," added Tubs.

Together, Zara and Caveman had begun a slow handclap accompanied by loud foot stamping.

Everyone grinned as Shane lifted up Snoog and was rewarded with a lick from a slurpy tongue that had just sampled somebody's milkshake.

"As I turned back to rescue this little fella..." he began.

Best say as little as possible about the Donn or how pumped up I was before sorting out those cloning scum – otherwise my friends might really think there is something weird about me...

174

Table of Contents